W9-BFR-688

Grandpa's Fiddle

Timothy James Halloran
2005

Author's Note

This work was inspired by a dream I had a few days before Thanksgiving in 1984. It involved a very old man telling me about himself. This dream was so vivid in my mind, that the next day I told my friend about this old man in the dream who touched me so deeply. He came again, this man, in subsequent dreams. This book is the fruit of those dreams and that man. Our country is the same, that old man's and mine. Our people are Americans. Our people are all races, all religions, and all Americans. For them and their ancestors, I finished this book. All stories contain certain myths. Within these myths there are fundamental truths about the human condition. I hope you will see them in my story, for that is what I attempted.

Acknowledgements

This author would like to thank and acknowledge the following individuals for their help and support.

To Christine, my colleague and friend who helped craft each and every word and patiently put up with all the edits. Thanks to Lynn P. who helped give me the confidence to write and to Tammy Hall, my musical inspiration.

To my wife and family, without whose love and support, I could not be who I am.

Many thanks to my editors, Jackie H. and Ellen Supple, who whipped it into shape. A special thanks to Dennis who first heard this story and whose artwork graces this book. For all of them and many more . . . go well, stay well.

Chapter I

Soldier's Tale

My daddy died on Christmas night in 1929. They say he caught consumption, or something or other. We had his laying-out three days later at Grady McMonigle's Funeral Parlor. Mama shook all over that night. She cried hard. So hard her sobs echoed in the parlor and made people look at each other in knowing glances. After lots of praying and standing and more praying, Mama took my sister Sarah, my brother Lincoln and me, William C, to see our grandpa.

Grandpa's name was Hoggen Cooper. My grandpa was the oldest man that I have ever seen in my ten years. Mama told me that Reverend Foster told her that grandpa was the oldest colored man in Chicago. If he wasn't, he sure must have been the second oldest, as far as I could tell. Anyways, Grandpa lived in a home for old soldiers on Washington Boulevard. It was up to us family to tell him about the funeral and all, 'cause Grandpa, he couldn't go. Mama said that Grandpa never went to no funerals as long as she'd known him. Grandpa told me once that he'd seen enough of men's corpses in the Civil War to suit him for his whole lifetime. No matter, folks at the parlor that night still whispered amongst themselves that it was awful that Grandpa didn't show up for his own son's funeral.

My brother, my sister and I had to wait out in the lobby by the front door of the home, which was fine with me. Except the whole place smelled like the camphor oil mama would rub on your chest to break your cough. We three Cooper children sat there with Linc rolling a cigarette, trying to act older than his fifteen years and he knowing how mama frowned on it.

Our grandpa had only been at the soldier's home for a few months. They took him there right after daddy took sick. Grandpa left the house one afternoon and started wandering in the city and got so lost that the police brought him home in the middle of the night. The policeman say they found him hobbling down Michigan Avenue in the middle of the night talking about his cane like it was a long rifle, said he was looking for his "Blackfoot" wife, Anna. We didn't see much of Grandpa after that. The house seemed so empty with his room still smelling of him and he not being there, plus Daddy being so sick that my brother and I would only come in for dinners most days.

The creaking door opened and mama came walking down the stairs and said that Grandpa wanted to see each of us children by ourselves in his room. Linc looked up and started walking up the stairs but she said no, it was Grandpa's wish to see me first cause I was the youngest.

Mama pushed open the swinging door of the great building and told me that Grandpa's room was down the hallway, "where the light was on," and I should "go see him right away and don't dawdle."

My dress shoes slapped on the floor as I walked. I could hear snoring sounds coming from the blackness of the rooms I passed. The hall was strewn with empty wheelchairs parked up against the wall and crutches and other such things to move them who don't have the legs they did have when they were born. The whole place smelled stale. The kind of stale that smells a place up that hasn't been opened up to the air so even the blankets and clothes is musty. Just as mama told me, there down the hallway on the right hand side was a light.

When I walked into the room, I saw Grandpa sitting up with a small light shining next to his bed. I hadn't realized how big the room was until I walked in. There I saw two rows of beds, five on each side, but Grandpa's was the only bed with the light shining on it. My grandpa was a thin, black, fine gentleman and sitting on his lap was his fiddle. An old hand carved fiddle that Grandpa would play at family gatherings, but especially on his birthday, which he claimed was the fourth of July, but nobody really knew it for sure.

Grandpa couldn't see too well, even though he had them thick round glasses that made it look like his eyes were bulging out when he looked you straight on. He had watery eyes that night, and I knew he'd been crying. When he saw me, he smiled and held out his long dark caramel hands and whispered, "Come here, now, Willy my boy. Don't you talk too loud, son, or you'll wake up the fellas." When I looked at my grandpa's arms I could see the long veins rising off and meandering down his thin wrinkled arms like rivers on a map.

Grandpa always kept his fiddle in a soft satiny sack in his room, and when they hauled him off to the old soldier's home, I didn't know what had happened to it, but knowing how much he loved it, I knew it'd be with him. That night, he told me this story, and now I know why he loved it so.

At first, he began in a slow whispering voice, weak 'cause of his age in years, but as he told it, his voice became strong again, swirling back through his 96 years of life.

"Now, let's see, boy," he said, "this here is how it all started . . ."

Chapter II

Abraham's Barrels

Long before this family came to the city and became "city folk," we lived on the land and we farmed and hunted. We'd darn our own clothes, make 'um ourselves, too. We'd shoot to eat and farm to live. We Coopers came to the city only when it was time cause the world was changing such that the city was a better place for colored people to live and find work. Now, the first Coopers were frontiering folk who lived free. Free long before President Lincoln emancipated any Negro in this here country. It was a time before everything was so civilized. There was still magic in the land and people knew it. Yes, boy, people still had some touch to their old ways. Not like today. Weren't no cars nor streets. I was born free. As was your great uncle Willy and my older brother Samuel. Your family name is Cooper, and your great-grandfather, Abraham, was the first Cooper, whose name he took whilst still a slave in Savannah, Georgia. It was Abraham who learned to make barrels, and barrel makers was called coopers. He used the name in secret 'cause he wouldn't take nor call himself Turner, although if you go back you see that his invoice, it say Turner.

Master's name was Cannaught Turner. He had a plantation and a small stable. That is where Abraham's hands shaped and molded and made the barrels that helped make Turner a well-to-do owner for some years. All his life, even in old age, it was Abraham's strong hands you noticed. When he'd nail with his hammer, be it a shoe on a horse or a nail in a barn, you could see the strength and speed that made his barrels the best in Georgia. It was the barrel and the way he could make them that finally got him free. See, your Great-Grandpa knew the way to figure how to seal them barrels for water and for rum that the white man hadn't yet figured out. And when it was time for the barrels to be cured, way in the blackness of the night when all the plantation was asleep, Abraham would treat the barrels with his own special mixture, so as to bring the resin to the lip of the barrel ribs and make them tough against the salt air.

"Turner's barrels", as they were called, fetched a good sum and had a fine reputation. As that reputation grew, the white men from Boston came down to buy the formula. When them barrels was filled with rum, they'd travel a good long time. Now that was what the northern whites wanted. But Master Turner, of course, didn't know how Abraham was able to make these barrels. Like most white folk, Turner treated that what he owned like it was ignorant or worse, and it was only when he couldn't figure out how to steal that which was Abraham's, that he sat down and talked to him.

"Well, Abraham, I must admit that your barrel making has made me quite renowned up north, for the rum casks you make don't sour the rum on its way up to market and the distillers would like to buy the formula or buy you." Now there comes a point in every creature's life, be it man or beast, when God opens but one door and you gets one chance. This day was Abraham's chance, and instantly he took it.

"Well, Master Turner, I may just forget it and one day wake up and then, of course, I would be nothing to you, except what I can do in smithing your plantation. 'Course, if you sold me, the shock is gonna cause me to lose all the learnin' I has for the barrel, and seeing I've got no wife nor children, whipping me to death ain't no loss to this old world."

Master Turner nodded, "It's not your hands that have some craft to them, Abraham. I suspected that you, being a bright nigra, would possibly be willing to provide me with that formula in exchange for you sharecropping a piece of my land and me, of course, giving you the pick of my plantation women to be yours." Like a lot of slave owners, Turner was constantly in need of money. He'd work his land for cash crops, spoil the soil, and when the land would fail, move to new land, taking on a new mortgage.

Sure, too, Turner knew well, as he heard the scuttlebutt from the kitchen slaves, that Abraham had his eye on Sarah, who worked in the main house. Now Abraham was tempted, yes he was, but he knew he would only get this one chance, so he took it. "Master Turner, you know the attorney, Mr. Stein, whose office is in Savannah over Miller's Dried Good?"

"Why, of course I know him," said Mr. Turner. "What of him?"

"If you was to have him draw up something to free me, I believe you and me and the Yank rum men could make ourselves a deal." Now, foxes don't like to swim but they will if they hungry 'nough. Why they'd swim across a river to catch a chicken. Well, Master Turner he needed that money real bad or he woulda lost his land. So, like the hungry fox, he crossed the river.

On that day in August, in the heat and humidity of a Georgia afternoon your Great Grandpa, the slave, horse traded himself to be a free man. Turner received $3,000 for the barrel making process, Abraham did as he said and showed them his secret, and the Yanks drank sweeter rum that winter on them cold Boston nights.

Chapter III

The Contract

Turner kept his word too. One week later, Abraham spent the morning putting on his best Sunday clothes. He walked very careful and solemn-like up to the door of attorney Stein's office. He took a breath, exhaled and then knocked on the door. He could hear the sounds of rustling papers and hard-booted footsteps, and braced himself as Stein opened the door. "Ah, it is you, Abraham," said attorney Stein in a very formal tone. "Come, come into my office and let us sit and talk." Stein did not talk like the other whites that Abraham was used to, nor did he dress like them. He had heard good things about Stein and he was glad that this gentleman would help make this document.

Stein said to Abraham in a hushed tone, "Now, Abraham, this document will be duly recorded in the county records of Georgia, so that your emancipated status will be public record." He then pointed out to the street. "You know, Abraham, I'm always pleased to help you negroes in this fashion. As you know, my inclination is against that slavery. God help me, I know my people have been enslaved enough through history."

Abraham nodded his head, "Yes sir, Mr. Stein. All of us do know of your feelings, though I believe no white man beside yourself would give a copper penny to help free a slave here."

Stein frowned and shook his head. "Ah, yes, Abraham. Some day it may be different."

After a pause, Abraham said, "Mr. Stein, may I ask one more thing of you? Would you read me what it say, for I can't read nor write."

Squinting his eyes, Stein smiled, which showed off broad, deep creases in his face. He took out his gold rimmed glasses, placed them on his long nose and said, "Of course, Abraham, how foolish of me not to read out loud that which is so dear to you." And so, Stein stood up and in a clear baritone voice read this paragraph.

"In accordance with the laws of the State of Georgia, County of Julian, this fourteenth day of September, 1821, that one Cannaught D. Turner, has duly and legally exercised his right to emancipate one male negro by the name of Abraham Turner now called Abraham Cooper, in due consideration, and in binding contract, for the delivery of $3,000 payment acknowledged and received by Turner, for delivery by one negro Abraham, to Northern Massachusetts Executor's Exchange, the curing process and method of cure of barrels. Signed and witnessed this day of our Lord, September fourteenth, 1821, signed Cannaught Turner witness hereof Attorney Stein."

"He really signed it, sir?"

"Yes, he did, Abraham."

Stein looked up. There was a tear running down Abraham's face. "Thank you. Thank you, Mr. Stein. You know, this is the first I used Cooper as my real name." Silence swallowed up the room, and as the darkly-dressed Stein stood behind his desk and stared at Abraham, he extended his hand.

"It's a fine name, Abraham. Good luck to you. Whatever you do, do not lose this paper. It is your only evidence of you being free. And I might also suggest that you leave this county as quickly as you can." "This is no place for free Negroes, not yet."

"Thank you, sir, Mr. Stein" said Abraham in a quiet tone. "I expect that's what I'll do, but I ain't yet fixed on where or how I'm gonna get to where I'm gonna go." Abraham took the extended hand and shook it firmly. He looked Stein in the eye and nodded his head. Looking a white man in the eye was a foolish thing, but he looked right at Stein anyway. This was something that he had been taught not to do, even as a child. Stein knew the importance of the look, and smiled warmly and nodded again.

With the papers in hand, Abraham stepped out into the morning Georgia sunshine. He still looked like a slave, even with his freedom in hand. The people looked at him as if they saw nothing else. He didn't know how to act otherwise in this world. To act any different, why that would bring the whole white wrath on him and he was not willing to act no different in this part of the country.

As long as he could remember, Abraham had the idea and the dream to find some freedom. That's what all of 'em wanted and needed. Just like a leaf turns towards the sun, Abraham's spirit guided him towards freedom. He walked slowly back to Turner's plantation. In the three miles it took to walk, he looked upon the land he passed, knowing it was going to be a farewell from all that was familiar to him. He smelled the pines, the grass, saw the familiar faces and fields. He walked by friends, all of whom, through the 'picket', had heard of his getting free. Some even singing out to cheer to him, but only if the owners or overseers weren't in shouting distance.

Abraham knew it wasn't worth no whipping for some field hands, but was happy when he heard their shouts. Thing is, Turner himself was talked down for freeing Abraham in the way that he did. Every free negro was a threat, but when the crops went bad and he needed the money, Turner took his cue from need, not no parlor manners.

When he got to the plantation, Abraham went to his small working shed. Inside he found young twelve year old Tom, who brightened as he saw Abraham walk through the door. "Whatcha gonna do, Mr. Abraham?" said Tom, in an inquisitive look. "My mama said ya gonna work for wages for Mr. Turner and maybe take you a wife. You think you can teach me 'bout barrel makin' too?"

He looked down kindly at the little boy, "I don't know, Tom, I will teach you what I can, just like I was taught by Old Nate, but I'm not sure Master Turner is ever goin' to get himself into another situation where he goin' ta need to sell a cooper's trick to keep his plantation." He and the boy both laughed at that.

Abraham put his apron on and started to work, more out of the need to do something rather than a compulsion to get anything done. Abraham needed time to think and to plan. Working his skilled hands on making horseshoes for 'Emilia,' Master Turner's prime mare, helped sharpen his thoughts as to what his next plan would be.

As he was working the hammer on the anvil in quick, strong strokes, the hair on his back stood on end. He could feel something or someone behind him. It was the same feeling all living creatures possess when something dangerous was about them, something which either hated them or wished them harm. Abraham turned around defensively, just like a deer sensing a wolf close by.

Ike Clemmer was a fat man with a sweaty face, spotty red skin and big meaty hands. He wore knee high boots and had a whip on his belt which he displayed always as a warning to those who would not abide his demeanor.

Clemmer stood and spat his name, "Abraham."

"What can I do for you, Sir?" Abraham used his field Negro voice when he spoke to Ike Clemmer, the plantation's overseer. He hated Clemmer with a passion so deep he sometimes lost reason. While Clemmer did oversee him directly, their interactions had been few. Clemmer knew nothing of smithing and Turner needed Abraham's barrels. Abraham knew Clemmer hated the fact that he could not control Abraham in the fashion he did the other slaves.

Clemmer spoke like a snake would if it had a voice, real whinny-like, "So, you a free nigger, huh, Abraham? How's it feel to be almost like a white man?" Clemmer said this but did not wait for an answer. "You listen here, Abraham. You need to leave this place, nigger. I don't want you here no more."

Abraham stood without moving. "I will be sure to tell Master Turner, sir, when I speak to him today," said Abraham, in a flat, serious voice.

Clemmer was quick to prey on the weaknesses of others to get his strength. But even in this place, alone in the shed with this now free man, he was not ready to take on Abraham alone. Clemmer was the type who would come in the night with others. Abraham knew this, and it drew his fury to know that he could not strike this man.

"You abide what I say," said Clemmer. "I should take this bull whip out now but . . . ," he hesitated, "you know about the boys. . ."

Abraham knew. They always came in packs like dogs to hunt down a runaway.

For the second time that day, Abraham looked a white man in the eye, straight in the eye, but his gaze weren't no gaze of

11

respect he showed Mr. Stein. It was raw and it was the hatred that good has of evil. Clemmer saw it too, and though he had, at first, reacted by grabbing at his whip, Clemmer didn't have the stomach for the battle. No, sir, and Abraham did not want to hang from no tree that day for killing a white man, either, but if it came to it, he would.

Clemmer, knowing that, backed away. "You abide me, now," he kept saying. "You abide me." At that, Clemmer turned and walked quickly out of the shed. Abraham's hand still clenched his hammer and his arm trembled. The hammer was like an extension of him, and it too pulsed with his anger.

Abraham took a deep breath, Now he knew he must have a plan.

As the afternoon turned into evening, Abraham walked out to the pond behind the field to think. The run in with Ike that morning had confirmed for him what had to happen. As the crickets sounded their evening knell and the light veil of the evening began to turn the green colors to grey, Abraham was sad. He knew that this place where he was born, despite all of its ugliness, had been his only home. Sure enough, though, it could no longer stay him. It was here that his mama, Reena, lived, blind as she was, and where his father, Bud, who'd been found in the pines, a murder still unexplained and unpunished, was buried. He loathed and yet loved this land. He felt like a man floating on the sea, clinging to a small raft. It was the only raft he had, and therefore, he clung tight to it. But in order to be truly free, Abraham had to swim away from it. That night he set out his plan to do so.

Sunday was the day that folks could gather and no work was required. Here, the worship of the Lord could take place, and on the Turner plantation that day, there was a great gathering of friends, family and community who all wanted to know what Abraham was gonna do.

Though simply clothed, these folks was always fresh and clean as they could make themselves, and they would all bring food to share. Course, there was laughter and singing, too. There was preaching that day of the promised land and Moses, and when he said the name Moses, Luther, who preached that day, nodded towards Abraham. "Amen," they all said in glee to Abraham, "Amen." The food tasted extra good to Abraham. Later he had a chance to walk over and talk with Sarah. He'd always thought she was a beautiful girl and now she had blossomed into womanhood. As far as he knew, she was "for him" from the moment she had turned fifteen, some years before.

Sarah, of course, was of an age when girls is skittish and flirty 'cause of men's natural inclination towards fawning all over them. She had heard of Abraham's freedom, and was as glad of it as she was glad of it for anyone.

"Abraham, this must be such a fine day for you."

"Why, yes, it is!" said Abraham. "Might I ask, Miss Sarah, what is it you do for yourself that makes your skin glow in such a beautiful manner?"

She laughed, "Mr. Abraham, I believe you're talking with such a honey-toned voice that it makes me question why you sayin' what you sayin'."

"I see what I see," he said. "I only tell the truth. How come you not married, Miss Sarah?" he asked, in a direct manner which even surprised him.

"Why, Abraham," she said, "you sure do go directly, now. Who would want to marry a little girl like me? I'm barely in my womanhood."

"You ought to be with a good man," he said.

"I will wait for the right one."

Sarah was five-foot- three, with a round figure and wonderful brown skin and an unblemished face. Fortunately for her, Mrs. Turner kept a tight rope around her white man or Sarah would already have been receiving night visits. The kind which she had heard others so frequently had on other plantations. It was enough to try and keep the overseer away and fortunate that she worked in the house and not in the field.

"I have dreams," Abraham said to her in a low tone, looking into the sky. "I would like you to be a part of them."

"You dream of what? Moving North?"

"No. I dream of living on my own land. I see a little creek with many wild flowers blooming in the spring. A place of my own to work and raise my family. Sometimes, Miss Sarah, if I close my eyes at night, I can smell the earth. Fresh plowed, on this farm that is mine."

Sarah smiled. Dreams were not a thing most people talked of when they spoke at Sunday get-togethers. The only dreams that slaves had were the dreams that came with the night and sleep, the dreams of heaven and a place after death.

"I will find a way," said Abraham. "Sarah, if you want me to, I'll take you with me. If you will wait."

Sarah's breath was taken away at first. She admired this man, who had such vigor, strength and spirit, and at that moment she knew that it was right. So she nodded her head and lowered her beautiful long lashes, saying, "I will wait for you."

Just then, Tom came running up to ask Abraham some questions and broke the moment between the two, which was, as far as Abraham was concerned, a relief. He said, "You take care, Miss Sarah," and she nodded back.

Monday morning, Turner came into the shed where

Abraham was cleaning up. "Abraham, now that you're a free nigger, I guess it's time to discuss about you staying on here as a wage earner."

"I expect," said Abraham, "that since Ike Clemmer wouldn't want me around much anyway, I'm gonna try and go find myself a job, maybe up in Charleston."

Turner sighed out loud, kinda disappointed. Then he said abruptly, "All these tools here are mine," he said, "don't you be taking those tools."

Abraham stared down at the ground.. He never took anything that didn't belong to him his whole life, but here was this man warning him of not taking that which was not his. But that same man himself had taken other men's freedom.

"Why, of course, Master Turner," he said. "I will just take these clothes on my back and what bundle I can of the rags I have collected, if you don't mind."

Turner's voice softened up once he realized how silly he sounded. "Why, of course, Abraham. You know I will miss you. You is a good worker. Why don't you go up to see Martha at the house. She will get you some food so you could be on your way. But if you change your mind, you know I would still pay your wage if you wish to stay, although I couldn't afford much."

"Thank you again, Master Turner," Abraham said, "but I will be on my way."

Abraham walked over to see his mama that morning, and held her tightly and kissed her, and whispered low into her ear. "Mama, I'm comin' back. I'm gonna come back for you, too."

But Mama Reena got real mad. "Don't you ever come back!" she said. "Don't ever come back. Let me die here knowin' you be free. That's what I want most. Don't ever come back!"

His mama only survived by the givin' of the other slaves in the plantation, for she was now useless to the owner except for the knitting she could do. Even so, her hands worked fast and true. She made good knots, but she needed others to help her with the stitching, which her friend and chief house cook, Martha, did lovingly.

With his eyes welling up with tears, Abraham walked off the plantation, one small man between the rows of tall trees planted on either side of the road. When he reached the end of the road, he looked back and saw Sarah in the distance. She waved at him, and he smiled and waved back. Then she turned and ran back toward the house. But that wave. Well, for Abraham, it was like a breeze on a calm ocean; that wave was like a puff of wind that fills the sail of a ship long stalled; and sure enough, it blew him through two weeks of walking and hitching rides all the way to the City of Charleston, a port city the likes of which Abraham hadn't ever seen before.

Charleston, South Carolina, was a hustling, bustling port city, whose docks were filled with cargo from all over the world. Cotton, molasses, rum and grain goin' north. The exotic smells all mixed with the ocean air.

Abraham wanted to go north, and he tried to find work to pay for his passage. He asked around the docks for anyone who needed labor. He received offers to load and unload cargo, which he did, and he received his first pay for wage in his whole life.

With five coppers in his pocket, he bought bread still warm from the bakers' ovens. Outside, he lit upon the most curious looking individual he had ever seen in his whole life. Outside this bakery under a huge shade tree stood a negro who must have been six foot, six inches tall with a bald head, leather vest, knicker-like trousers and tall black boots. He had scar-like tattooes running in weaving patterns up and down his arms. The big man also had a most exotic looking tattoo on his bare chest.

In a baritone, deep voice with a most funny way of talkin', he said to Abraham, "What you are looking at?"

Abraham was startled. "What is it you have on your arms? What kind of scars have they given you?"

He laughed a loud laugh, "I call these my scrimshaws," he said. "This is who I am."

Abraham peered closer and pointed to the great man's chest, "What is that on your chest?"

"This is the tattoo from the Karankawas. It was made for me by one of the last living Karankawas on the island of Malhado. You see, he saved me from a shipwreck. I was a young sailor then. I couldn't even swim and I was drowning in the water off of Machado Island when he pulled me into his boat. I became like his son. He taught me so much that I shave my head as he did and the tattoo, I wear it proudly to remember him. They are a people no more," Scrimshaw said sadly. "Killed by disease from the whites."

"What is it? It looks like a dog or a wolf."

"Yes! Good for you! It is, for they were known as the dog people. That was their animal spirit. They were a very tall people. Yet, my new friend, among them I was not tall. His name was Elso, he was this much taller than me." And at that Scrimshaw raised his hand six inches above his head.

"They were giants, then!" said Abraham.

"Yes, but no more. Gone like leaves from the tree in winter."

Abraham changed the subject when he saw he was making the big man look sad. "Where are you from?" he asked. "I have never seen a negro like you before."

"They call me Scrimshaw. I'm from many places. And you, little man, where are you from?" smiled the giant.

"I'm a free negro from Georgia. My name is Abraham, Abraham Cooper." He extended his hand.

"Ah," said Scrimshaw. "What puts you here in this port city?"

"I'm looking for work. I need to get work to start my new life."

"Life," said Scrimshaw, "it is a most peculiar state, is it not? Life?" Scrimshaw sat down next to Abraham. "Let me tell you about life."

Scrimshaw broke bread with Abraham and began to tell him of his life. He told him about Africa and how he received the ceremonial scars along his arms as part of the journey into manhood to identify what spirits he would take. He then went on about how he was enslaved and his hellish passage to the Caribbean. There was years of working on cane plantations and finally the lucky day that he was sold as a slave ship worker and the places he traveled and the people he saw in the wondrous world. Scrimshaw spoke of the Yankee captain who eventually let him buy his freedom. Scrimshaw told Abraham about the years he spent on the sea, carving ivory tusks on long nights on the ocean. He proudly displayed a scrimshaw tusk he had carved and Abraham was awed at the beauty of it.

"I guess that's where you got your name?" said Abraham inquisitively.

"Yes, of course! That's where I got my name."

"Why did you not go back to Africa, where you were from?" asked Abraham.

"I have been. But my home now is the sea."

When Abraham explained how he had become free,

Scrimshaw laughed. "So, you are a barrel-maker?"

"Yes, and a smith, too," Abraham said proudly. "I could forge anything, if ya give me the right tools."

"My ship has tools. She's the Alabaster docked over there. If I ask Captain McGorg if he is in need of a good smith, and he is, you'll be the one. The wage is paid by the voyage. You'll never work so hard nor be so sick, but you'll see the ports and sea and worlds that you may never ever see again," said Scrimshaw. "Come now, I'll buy you some rum, and we'll talk more."

Abraham was not a drinking man, but at that point, he was enjoying this Scrimshaw and his stories, so he imbibed in a lot of rum and laughter. Abraham had never had such a good time in his whole life. He woke up in a room that Scrimshaw had been letting, and his head felt as if a wagon wheel had rolled over it. He was thirsty and dry-tongued. He drank water directly from the pitcher on a nearby table.

Later that morning, they went to the Alabaster and talked with Captain McGorg. In a fortnight, after more days and nights of having Scrimshaw show him the carnival-like world of the Charleston port, he set sail on his first sea voyage.

The Alabaster was heading north to deliver cargo to Boston harbor, and though he was seasick the first day and a half, his sea legs gradually came upon him.

Abraham was given a quick and rude education of life on the sea. The sailors were a mixed bunch of coarse, hard, white men who kept to themselves, and some freed negro and Cuban sailors. Captain McGorg was a serious man who laughed little, and yelled a lot. His first mate, Roger Bowman, insisted upon everyone being constantly busy throughout the entire voyage to Boston.

Abraham's hands were strong from his work in the forge with a hammer, but were made raw from the rope-work and climbing, at which he was very new. But he'd never felt so free in his life, for here men treated each other as men and had to work as a team or die as a group. Each man's job was as important as the other's when it came to trimming sail, making fast with rope, fixing the broken harness, and setting a course that would be true and not lead to the rock or bottom of the ocean.

Abraham could see why Scrimshaw had adopted this as his home. For here it was only nature, the smell of the air and the hard work and focus of doing the job.

The Alabaster was a three-masted ship and she was fast. In no time they were in Boston harbor. Abraham was excited to see this new city he'd heard so much about growing up. Yes, sir, for it was the north. That's what all slaves heard would be the place for them.

'Course, what Abraham had not realized was when he signed up for the ship's job, because he couldn't read, he had signed for a two-year voyage. Though they stopped in Boston to unload and reload, and while he was keen to the look of the Yankee white folk and the apparent freedom that a negro free man could have there, Abraham had obligated himself under contract to another man for work. Abraham just wasn't a man who'd break his promise.

After they set sail again from Boston harbor, Abraham asked the first mate about their next port. When he heard, he was in some ways happy that he had held to his bargain. "We're sailing to Africa!" said Bowman.

"Africa," said Abraham. It was as if a call came from deep, deep, deep within his own self that had finally echoed off the walls to reach his ear. "Africa."

And so it was this: Abraham would go to Africa, far differently than when his grandfather was chained and taken from there. Abraham thought long and hard on this subject, and talked at great length about it with Scrimshaw and about what he might find in the home of his ancestors.

Chapter IV

Home, Africa

Scrimshaw's home was the ocean. He had sailed its seas, visited exotic islands off the coast of the Orient, and sailed around the horn of Africa. Scrimshaw was 56 years old, but the muscles on his body were hard and no man on the ship was stronger. Having no family of his own, Abraham became like a son. They would talk for hours when their work was done. For three straight weeks, Abraham, Scrimshaw, Johnny Timmans, Raul Lopez and Deke Mobley, engaged in a ranting, screaming, shouting game of penny card poker.

Abraham never before enjoyed the company of men such as these. Deke Mobley was a thin, wiry, strong man from Tennessee. Lopez from Santa Maria Island, and Timmans from Connecticut. At the center of it all was Scrimshaw. He was the one who told tall tales and read men's fortunes by throwing his bones and peering at them and twisting his head back and forth, as he gazed at them.

Abraham asked Scrimshaw one evening after the penny poker game was done, "Where'd you get them bones that you throw down there?"

"They were given to me by a voodoo princess," said Scrimshaw. "She was most powerful. She had much in knowledge. She could cast a spell on a man and turn him to . . . well, you don't want to know." Scrimshaw chuckled, "Some things best not said at all. But the power in these bones be strong, and these bones tell tales, and fortunes too."

"I'm a Christian man," said Abraham, "and don't believe in such things."

"There are things of this earth," Scrimshaw pointed toward the deck, "and there are things of the sky. Your God is the God of the sky," and he looked up at the stars. "These things in my hand are of the earth. You should heed their call."

"Why did you come on this voyage?" Scrimshaw said suddenly. "You long for your woman, if you can call her that, and yet you sail home to your grandfather's country."

Abraham had been thinking about that a lot himself.

"Scrimshaw, I have an ache in me. I can't explain it. I don't know what it is. I feel like I'm going home, but my mama and daddy seldom talked about Africa, except maybe on a Sunday."

"I'll throw the bones for you. We'll find out if this is a voyage and adventure or pilgrimage." In the lantern light in the galley, Abraham said no to the invitation. Not wanting to insult his friend, he simply said it would be best that they do it some other day. But after that night, he continued to think long and hard as the ship rolled back and forth on the seas and he attended to his duties. Sure, he was being paid, and the captain was a fair man, but he knew he could have stayed in Boston, gotten work, perhaps for more money, so he could get the sums to get his Sarah, and start his life. So why had he gone on this voyage?

There were strong tradewinds blowing, and it weren't longer than a few of months before, they reached the west coast of Africa. "Land ho!" cried Mobley, who was in the crow's nest, a welcome sight for any sailor who had been at sea for a long time. Once in the port, the crew knew there would be grub, ale, and adventure. For no sailor heeds the sea only for the smell of the salt air, not surely, but also for the adventure of a new port.

23

"Abraham, do you know what this was like ten years ago? This country still allowed slave trading. Then the British outlawed it in 1807. Before that time," Scrimshaw grimaced, "you could hear the groans and moans of our people squeezed into little sling rows of the evil devil ships. It was bad fortune for a merchant ship to cross its path. We avoided them."

Hearing these tales boiled the blood in Abraham. "I hope to God there's a hell for them that ruin so many lives."

"It is evil in men's hearts, and that evil has no color. It is greed and avarice," said Scrimshaw. "I try to look to a man's heart first before I judge him on anything else, you see."

"Yes, I do," Abraham said. "I guess we all should do that."

With the sails coming down, Abraham looked into the Port of Koadoa. There he saw people in long robes of many colors. They were muslims black of skin. They were long, thin people. There were turbaned laborers on the docks and the smells were unlike any he'd ever smelled before. Scrimshaw put his arm on Abraham's shoulder as they watched the moorlines being tied off.

"Home, Africa," said Scrimshaw as he spread his arms out. "This is the home of your people and mine. There is beauty here, and treachery, laughter and adventure."

Having been given some shore pay by the bosun, Scrimshaw was ready for an adventure.

"Abraham," said Scrimshaw, "just down the road there is an ale shop. The best African beer, sweet-smelling women and wonderful roast fowl."

But Abraham wanted to make his first step onto the soil of Africa a quiet, thoughtful occasion. He wanted it to mean something. But before he knew it, Scrimshaw, Lopez and Mobley were chattering and badgering, talking about where they were going to go and what they were going to do. He had lost the moment and got pulled down the gang plank before he could collect his thoughts.

For a split moment, his thoughts turned to Sarah. His Sarah. He thought about whether she still thought of him; if she had give up and married another or whether Turner had sold her and sent her away. These were the thoughts he had many times at sea, and as he stood upon the land of her ancestors as well, he wondered what she would be like here. Would she look like the women he saw with bracelets and lapid eyes and veiled smiles?

The crew, his friends, drank heartily that night. Abraham admired how they reveled in their sense of who they were. Early the next morning, Abraham opened his eyes looking skyward on the gray dawn in the Sierra Leon port city, his head pounding.

He sat up suddenly. "Scrimshaw! Scrimshaw!" called Abraham, unsure of where he was. Leaning against the wooden shed, Scrimshaw with his arm around a portly woman, blinked lazily.

"You still alive, Abraham?" said Scrimshaw. "I saw you drop. I thought maybe you died!" They laughed a headache laugh, and stretched and yawned, and then Scrimshaw said farewell to his woman friend.

"You sending me down a bad road," Abraham said.

"A bad road?" said Scrimshaw. "You are a sailor, man, and have come to port to celebrate your successful voyage. It is the ceremony of a sailor."

"But I have come here to learn."

"And learn you have, Abraham," said Scrimshaw. "and I will throw my bones for you today, and you will learn more."

At that point, the great man squatted in the red dust of the village, and whispering an incantation which Abraham could not understand, he threw little white bones onto the dusty soil. Creasing his brow, he read the fall of the bones and they way of their criss-crossing. There was a long pause and silence.

"Well," said Abraham, "what do you see, man?"

"Mmmm," said Scrimshaw. "Interesting"

"Well?" said Abraham. "What is it? Am I here to stay? Am I here to go? Am I here to make my fortune?"

"Mmmm," said Scrimshaw again. "Very interesting."

"Scrimshaw, I'm gonna knock you up on your bald head if you don't tell me what you seein'."

"Shhh," he said, "you are not here for the purpose that you think." There was more silence.

Abraham was exhausted with the tension of the silence. "Tell me what it says!"

"You come here thinking Africa is yours, but she is not. You come here to get something. A tool, a symbol."

"What is it?" asked Abraham.

"I can't tell you. But the bones, they say you will know it when you find it. You will pay what price you must for it. It will mean something for you. What, I cannot tell you."

"You must be some crazy man!" Abraham muttered. "Well, where's it say I have to go?"

"I cannot tell you."

"That's it! You strange man, Scrimshaw," said Abraham.

"Also," said Scrimshaw pausing, and the silence continued.

"Also what?" Abraham asked. "Also what, Scrimshaw?"

"You will find your home somewhere along a great river."

"Yeah?" said Abraham. "Where?"

"I have lost sight," said Scrimshaw. "Maybe it was the ale we drank last night." At that, the man picked up the bones in his great hands and put them in his vest pocket. He was sweating from his concentration and from no food or water, so they set off to find a place to eat.

As they walked, Abraham was daydreaming about his entry into Africa, seeing villagers and sensing what life must have been like for his ancestors, and the sweet and spicy exotic smells of the people and this earth. He wondered what village his grandfather had been in, and was angered about that which had been taken from them. Though he was in an African city and an African port, he nevertheless saw, even heard, the influence of the European: the European way and dress. He even looked to these Africans as a foreigner.

His daydreaming was suddenly disrupted by the slap on his back by Scrimshaw. "Where are you?" asked Scrimshaw. "You are the most dreaming man I ever seen. Come, we must go to the bazaar. You can find anything you desire in that market-place."

And so the two men walked into the confusion and noise of the bazaar. Smells were everywhere: sweetened meats, carpets, vegetables, chickens, hides, everything that could be sold or dis-covered was there. Still hurting from the previous night and the overbearing heat of the African sun which was so much differ-ent in Georgia, Abraham took a small alley and tried to find some shade.

Abraham chuckled to himself when he thought of Scrimshaw telling him of the great, powerful item that he must purchase that would symbolize something for him. He had since spent half of his money the night before carousing with his friend. He leaned his head up against an adobe wall and, taking deep breaths, tried to relax. When he opened his eyes, across from him he saw an Arab gentleman in a long tunic outfit and hat. The man was smoking and watching the smoke drift up into the sky. He was standing in front of what appeared to be a small shop of all sorts of items. In perfect English, the marketer said, "I'm glad you've come."

Lifting his head from the wall, Abraham looked both ways, thinking perhaps the man had been speaking to someone else. "Sir?" said Abraham. "Are you speaking to me, sir?"

"Yes. I'm glad that you've come."

"What do you mean?"

"Well, this is an excellent day for you to shop. Come into my place. I have many good buys for you, sir."

Taken aback by the man's trading spirit, Abraham got up and stretched himself. "I am Abraham," he said, extending his hand to the man.

"I am Fahid," the man said as he grasped Abraham's hand.

"Fahid," said Abraham, "I'm not really here to purchase anything, but I'm glad that you asked me to step into your shop and look."

"You have the look of a man who is in search of something," said Fahid. "Perhaps your search will end here." The store was dusty and there was a brassy smell from the pipes that were lining one wall. The wood smells from the masks and the hand carved items within made Abraham think of home. Carpets were in a pile on the floor, and behind the counter there were knives and swords, all of which were most beautiful, and Abraham couldn't help but gaze at them.

"A man like you should think about a purchase such as this," said Fahid as he lifted up a long sword.

"I have no use for weapons."

"Art!" said Fahid. "A man like you should have art."

"I have no use for this art, although it is beautiful."

"You have a wife? Children?"

"No," said Abraham. "I am alone."

"Ah," said Fahid, "alone. Then this, I must show you. For when a man is alone, he is in need of company." At that, Fahid went to the back of his small store and came back with a silk sack. "This," said Fahid, "is what you need."

Unwrapping the silk sack, Abraham saw that there was a maple-colored fiddle with a bow. It was shiny but pockmarked from time, usage and wear. "I purchased it from a British soldier who had, because of a recent string of bad luck, been unable to meet the cash needs of his creditors."

"I don't play an instrument," said Abraham.

"It is more than an instrument. An instrument properly played in the proper hands becomes an extension of you," said Fahid. "Here, I will show you how to hold it."

Stepping behind Abraham, Fahid put the violin under Abraham's chin, put the bowstring in his hand, placing his fingers on the strings and had Abraham screech and squeal out sounds from this awkward instrument. At that moment, a great shadow engulfed the doorway of the small shop, and Scrimshaw, looking at Abraham standing there with the instrument under his chin, smiled. "I see you've found it," said Scrimshaw. "A most beautiful instrument."

"This couldn't be what you were talking about," said Abraham.

"Close your eyes," said Scrimshaw. Fahid, not knowing exactly what the two men were speaking of, stepped back, but understanding how sometimes a third party can help a sale, agreed. "Oh yes," said Fahid. "Close your eyes, Abraham. Think of the beautiful melodies you could play to the woman that you love. What you could do while you were alone making the sweet music. A most fine purchase it would be," said Fahid.

Abraham closed his eyes. The wood under his chin felt soft and hard at the same time; it had been fitted for the chin of a man such as he, he could tell, and though his strong, callused fingers could barely put the proper pressure onto the strings, he liked its feel. It was a silly purchase, he thought, and one which he couldn't afford in any event because he didn't have enough money. While Fahid told him the extraordinary price of the instrument, it was Scrimshaw who stepped into the deal making.

"This is worth nothing," said Scrimshaw. "I would barely give you a dollar."

"Please, sir, do not insult me. You know it is worth at least fifteen dollars."

"Nah! Let us go," said Scrimshaw to Abraham. "We will leave this place now. I saw a similar one just down the road."

"Nothing of this value! Nothing at all," the market man's voice got higher in pitch. "However, I wish to do gracious things for this man, for I can see that this is his."

"Seven dollars."

"Gold."

Abraham looked at Scrimshaw. "I've got two," he whispered.

"Here," said Scrimshaw, plopping down a small bag from his vest. "There is your money, good merchant. The sack goes with it."

"As you wish." And the market man handed him the fiddle. Scrimshaw winked at Fahid, and Abraham was soon walking out with no money in his pocket, and an instrument he could not play.

"This got to be the stupidest thing I've ever done," said Abraham. "Now I've got no money."

"Ah, but you have a fiddle. And you can practice on the ship all the way back," Scrimshaw shot back.

"All the way back?" asked Abraham.

"Yes, we sail in a week," Scrimshaw told him.

"But I barely had a chance to even see this . . ." He stopped.

"What is it you want?" asked Scrimshaw. "To spend a year here learning about this land, this wonderful land, or to earn enough to go back for this woman that you keep telling me so much about? This is the road you must take," said Scrimshaw to him in his deep voice. "But the road goes two ways. The ship sails soon. If you do not come, the gold was a gift for your instrument. If you do, you'll pay me back." Then Scrimshaw turned away and strode off into the dusty streets again, back to the bazaar.

Abraham's head was spinning. He'd hardly been in Africa and had spent the whole of money and was holding a silk sack with a violin that he couldn't play, and his only known way of going back to America was leaving soon and he'd seen so little of the country that he'd wanted to see.

His whole life, Abraham always secretly had his own plan for freedom. Now, thrown into the world as a free man with places to go and things to see and do, he was paralyzed by his own choices. That day he sat and he took out the violin. Putting his fingers on the strings, he started moving the bow across the strings, screeching, working awful sounds, but since no one was in the alley, he did not think he'd harm anyone's ears.

"If you want to do that, sir, I would request that you please stop doing that in front of my home." Abraham turned around to see a pasty white English gentleman standing in the doorway of a small, humble home where Abraham had squatted.

"Excuse me, sir. I just bought this fiddle and I am attempting to play it."

"That, sir, is not 'playing'. That, sir, is abusing one's ears!"

"I have no training and I just bought it."

"Nothing," said the gentleman, "excuses the kinds of sounds emanating from that instrument. Here, let me see. Hmm," said the gentleman, "where did you purchase this?"

"Around the corner, on the other side of the bazaar."

"A fine instrument. Here, let me show you something." At that, the Englishman stuck the violin under his chin, and placing his fingers on the strings, began to play a tune. He closed his eyes as he played, and Abraham could see that an instrument such as this, played properly, created a beautiful sound.

"Here," said the gentleman, "let me show you how to hold your fingers." And placing his fingers squarely across, and holding Abraham's hand across the bow, thus so, Abraham could hear the faintest, squealing sound of a real note played properly on his fiddle. "Charles Birmingham," said the gentleman, as he helped Abraham.

"Abraham Cooper."

"You're an American!"

"Yes," said Abraham. "I guess I am." It was the first time anyone had called him that.

Birmingham and Abraham had tea, and Abraham was treated to a proper British gentleman's day. Birmingham, was a widower who had been part of the foreign executor's office of the British colony. He was a lonely man, who was happy for the company of this new fiddler.

The music lesson made Abraham feel so good, he thought maybe Scrimshaw was right; the fiddle was the right thing to buy. But something more that Birmingham said made Abraham know that his course had been set long ago. Over and over in his head, he remembered the Englishman's words. "An American," he called Abraham. An American.

Chapter V

The Poker Game

The Captain was not a man who wasted time. When the ship was to sail at high tide at 8:00 in the morning, it sailed. Scrimshaw said many was the man who was left waving and wailing for the Captain to return to shore because of the mistaken belief that being a few minutes late of the proper time would still get a man on his voyage back. Abraham was there on time, and walking up the plank with the silk sack in hand, he saw Scrimshaw tying up some mizzen sail sheets.

"Ah," said Scrimshaw to Abraham. "What's in the sack?"

"What's in the sack?" said Abraham. "Good God, man, has the ale rattled your brain?"

"Ohhh," said Scrimshaw. "Of course. It's your fiddle. Can you play us a tune yet?" asked Scrimshaw.

"What's that?" Deke Mobley asked.

"It's my fiddle," said Scrimshaw.

"'Tis not," said Abraham. "It's mine."

Scrimshaw smiled and nodded. "Yes, . . . Yes, it is."

"Well, I can show you how to play some of that. I learned a bit of a fiddle myself when I was growing up," said Mobley.

"We'll have a fine voyage back," said Scrimshaw. Looking down from his vantage, Scrimshaw looked at Abraham and pointing out to sea, he said, "So your road goes this way."

"Yes," Abraham said, "I guess it does." When the ship sailed, Abraham stayed on deck and watched the land - the land of his fathers - until it disappeared from view in the blue Atlantic.

For Abraham, there was something reassuring about being back on the ship now. The pace of working calmed him down as the ship smith fixing the rigging or the pleat. Having his hands work on familiar things was reassuring. In the lantern candle-light of the small shop behind the galley with the help of Deke Mobley, who could read and write, Abraham Cooper carved on the back of his fiddle "AC" and the year "1822".

For the next seven days, a storm slashed and bashed the ship so badly that Abraham thought that perhaps he and his fiddle would end up at the bottom of the ocean. Sailors are generally a fun, happy-go-lucky lot, but at times like this, they were set-jawed and grim. They spoke little and worked hard, for it was absolute survival that was at hand. This wasn't no dilly-dally, soft breeze of a voyage. These men worked for survival, and Abraham was scared every day during the storm and rough seas, but never had he felt closer to any men than he did at that time. On the eighth day, the storm broke, and everyone took a deep breath. The crew relaxed itself, and the camaraderie and joking and bantering came back as they went about their work.

Loaded with spices, the Alabaster was heading to Jamaica, Boston, and then south to Savannah. Once again, the penny card games continued. Abraham practiced with his fiddle with Mobley teaching him the scales. The crew kept kidding Abraham that there were no albatrosses flying close to the ship because of "those noises" Abraham Cooper made with that damn fiddle of his. After months and months, Abraham was back in the South.

Once off ship, Scrimshaw, as usual, talked Abraham into going to Carney's Card Parlor to see if they couldn't increase the money they'd received on exiting ship.

"Abraham, it's time for you to play real cards."

"How come every time I get off a ship, you're ready to spend my money? I told you, I gotta save my money."

"Look, you still owe me five dollars," said Scrimshaw. "Let's see if you can get it playing cards with me."

Abraham always seemed to be thrown off his course by Scrimshaw. Before he knew it, Abraham was walking down Main Street to the shanty-shacks on the other side of the river. Yes, sir, the great Scrimshaw and his friend, Abraham, and a silk sack were in a card parlor before the sun had set.

As serious faced as the sailors were during the storm on the way back, so too were the men around this here card table. They were squint-eyed men with little cigars and broad hats, and it was a dollar ante for each player.

Abraham played his game cautiously, and was up a few dollars. Scrimshaw played the game with passion and laughter, and plenty of chatter that bothered the silent men around him, but when you were as big as old Scrimshaw, most men would not want to cross him or anger him. "This is a fine day," said Scrimshaw to the men, with no one in particular in mind. "A lucky, lucky day."

"Ante up," said the thin-mustached man doling out the cards, whose name was Rory. "Chatter is for women. This is cards."

Scrimshaw laughed. "Cards, cards, cards. How I love the cards." They were playing no-draw poker, and the white man, Rory, Abraham could tell, had taken a deep dislike to Scrimshaw's card playing. Oftentimes, in a game such as this, it was one man taking things too personal which led to crazy hands. Rory's anger over Scrimshaw's banter is exactly what begot this hand, which was the craziest of all.

"I'll see you one and raise you five," said Rory.

Scrimshaw looked at his cards and smiled.

"Fold," said the silver haired man next to him.

"Fold," said the white coated southern gentleman.

"See you," said Scrimshaw, "and raise you one." At that moment, Scrimshaw took the money which was in Abraham's pile and put it in. Abraham's face looked like Scrimshaw had just pulled his pants down.

"Wha—," was the only sound that Abraham could make. Scrimshaw nodded his head knowingly. "Fold," said Abraham.

"I see you that and raise you five."

This went on for some time, until finally Abraham, seeing that Scrimshaw had no more money, looked at him and whispered in his ear, "Scrimshaw, should we talk?"

"No talking," said Rory. "This is poker." The man called the last raise of twenty dollars, and triumphantly, was about to take in the pile of cash that was surrounding the remaining cards, when Scrimshaw reached over and, picking up the silken sack, placed it on the table. "I call with this fine, fine, Italian fiddle."

Abraham was choking on his words and he could barely speak. "Scrimshaw!" he finally said. "That's . . ."

" - mine," said Scrimshaw. "Remember? You still owe me for it."

Three randy jacks took the day over two aces. Fortunately for Abraham, them jacks were in the gigantic brown hand of his friend, Scrimshaw. Triumphantly, his friend wanted to play another hand to make this truly his biggest day ever, but Abraham was able to convince Scrimshaw to leave and calm down the poker player, Rory, enough so that they could all leave with his fiddle and $400. Of course, Scrimshaw split the money equally, since it was the fiddle, of course, that had won the day. Amazingly, the streak continued for two more days. Though Abraham almost choked and died from the tension of it all, Scrimshaw had turned the lucky streak into $1,000. But this time, though Scrimshaw continued to plead for Abraham to stay with him on the streak, Abraham refused, taking his money, and thinking perhaps that now of all times would be the time to go back for Sarah.

"Never leave a lucky streak, Abraham!" Scrimshaw said.

"It's time for me to go or I may never get a chance to get my woman."

"You risk a lucky streak for a woman you have not seen in two years? My friend, I'm not the gambler, you are!" Scrimshaw spat out. "Give me your hand," Scrimshaw said. "There is some more money to travel on with. My parting gift to you."

Abraham stared at his friend in amazement, "I can't say how much you mean to me, Scrimshaw. You are . . ."

"We came together for a reason, Abraham. We part for one, too. Perhaps we will see each other again, but if not, it has been a grand sail with you along."

At that, Scrimshaw clasped his arms around Abraham and squeezed him tightly. Abraham started walking, but turned one more time to wave good-bye, but Scrimshaw had already disappeared into another card parlor, vanishing quickly. As the last sliver of the sun set over the ocean, Abraham knew he would never forget Scrimshaw.

Sarah's Choice

It had been many months since Abraham had left. Sarah felt different after he was gone. "Girl, your body's here but your mind ain't," said the assistant cook Emily as she and Sarah shucked the corn for supper.

"Sometimes I think that sweet talk of Abraham was just that," said Sarah wistfully, "ain't no one ever goin come back and take me away from all this," she sighed.

"You a slave 'til they free you or God take you," Emily whispered, "but no Abraham from this county is goin' to take you girl to some promise land," she laughed. Sarah laughed too, because she knew that she had no control over whether Abraham came back or not.

Though she was busy, Sarah was lonely. At twenty-two she was considered old not to have a man or a baby and she had overheard talk by the other women. Overheard talk of other men too. Charles at the Walker plantation had wanted her to jump the broom and had asked her on many occasions. He was a fine looking, strong man and most women would have taken him to their bosoms. Sarah remembered the last time they had spoken.

"Charles you honor me with your offer, but . . ."

"He ain't comin' back Sarah. Don't you know? Any body that got a chance to leave here, he ain't comin' back to this place."

Charles was passionate for Sarah and his passion for her clearly overcame his normally courteous manner.

"Sarah, you and I could steal away out of here. We could do it, you know."

But Sarah knew deep in her heart that Charles was not a man who would run away. The risks were great for a slave to run, and some simply would not risk their life for freedom.

Even more, Sarah remembered her promise to Abraham. It was funny though, for she was not drawn to him in a physical way. Abraham, was older and not as handsome as some men. But his eyes, she told Emily, his eyes were like liquid pools of spirit. That was what immediately attracted her to him. She desired only to see those eyes again and, of course, perhaps give her what she needed too, her freedom!

As they continued to shuck the corn, Emily again chided her, "all these months and nothing. My goodness, child, don't you think he would try and get a word to ya, if he possibly could or if he wanted to?" Of course, Sarah knew that it was true. There are ways. While the white man tried to keep you from book learnin' and writin', the slaves made their own way. Word got through, though often fractured and tortured, from farm to farm and plantation to plantation. A separated child could still get some word from a parent, usually it was talk across a fence or a road and especially talking with the pass in hand. When a master needed a slave to leave the plantation, he gave him a pass. Every man, woman and child could tell a tale and pass it on to another. But still no word from Abraham.

"You know," said Emily, "Ike said Abraham probably got hisself kilt."

"Do you think that's true miss?" little Tom yelled out. Silently listening this whole time, he looked up with such painful eyes that Sarah put her arm around him.

"I don't think so," said Sarah. "Abraham is a smart man. He

knows how to hold his tongue."

Emily turned to shuck more corn and Sarah said in a low voice, "Don't be sayin' that in front of Miss Reena. She's had a sorrowful enough life without you commentin' on rumors 'bout what may have happened to her boy."

It was three days later that something came, late one afternoon. Jordan, a driver for the Castle family had talked to Edgar, Turner's stable man, who stated that while Ms. Castle had been to Savannah for her sister's wedding and a shopping spree, he'd run into a houseboy by the name of Louis, who was talking to a man named Oscar. Oscar had seen Abraham at the docks when Oscar was down there getting some imported harness for his master. They got to talkin' and Abraham told him all about himself, and there you have it. And so, weaving up like a web, word of Abraham came out of the shadow of silence, spread back into the county, then to the farm and into the house where Sarah heard the word.

It was just this little bit of news, gave her the faith that she needed to continue her wait.

As always, Emily was the great examiner of Sarah. "Why is it that you want this man. You can still have Charles or some other. Charles, he really is a good lookin' man anyway," Emily said, betraying her own desires.

Sarah laughed, "You settle for the body. I'm settling for something else and I'm goin' to wait."

"Don't let the fruit hit the ground girl – it will rot!"

"Shhhh! Stop talkin' like that," Sarah scolded Emily.

Chapter VII

The Loving of Sarah

On his voyage, Abraham had heard of new openings of lands to the west. Men by the name of Lewis and Clark had charted up the great Mississippi River far into the north. They said it was a land of untold and unimagined riches. Abraham wanted land and if it was there, then that's where he was goin'. But first he had something more important to do.

It was late in 1823. Ahead of him, the thought of his journey back to the plantation was filled with dread, for Abraham did not know if the woman that he was going back for would even be there. Abraham never got no word that his letters written by Deke Mobley ever got through.

Abraham had done one thing in hopes that he could show Sarah what she meant to him. He purchased a broach for her. He wanted it to be her wedding gift. It was wrapped in a sack, safely tied on his waist.

Abraham had walked out of that land of his slavery, but he would ride back on a rickety swayback horse which he had purchased from a toothless horse trader by the name of Braxton.

The journey back was twice as hard not just because he didn't know what awaited him there, but because he would have to leave Scrimshaw behind.

Abraham was thinking about this on his way out of town when he heard a loud yell from behind. "Whoa, my friend, not so fast! I know it is your time to go, but we didn't leave right.

You are like my son and . . . the cards went bad last night."

Abraham grabbed each of Scrimshaw's long forearms and held them tightly, "There has never been a friend like you, Scrimshaw. You have taught me more than any man I know, except the man who taught me my Smithing. I wish you would come with me. Will you?" Abraham asked earnestly.

"I am a seafaring man," Scrimshaw said. "The sea is my home. The river that you seek, I think you know now, must be the Mississippi. The land you seek I do not know, nor how you will find it, or where it will lie, but I bid you my best. Shall I throw the bones for you one more time?"

Abraham sighed, "If you think I need it, do so now, before I regret it and say no." And so once again, the great black man kneeled on his haunches and then shook the bones. His great hands hovered over the bones, then his eyes squinted and his lips got tight. Real tight.

"I cannot tell you all because . . . well, some of this is about me. But harm will come your way. Both death and a new life."

"Death?" said Abraham.

"And new life," said Scrimshaw. "There will be a woman who will give you new life. There will be a man who will die and you shall give him rebirth. I say no more."

Abraham was shaken by the words of Scrimshaw and Scrimshaw felt it.

"Let's talk no more of this, my friend. The bones sometimes mean nothing that we think, but mean something else. Come, let's drink rum before you leave. It should be as seamen say, 'good-bye and fair sailing' and we should think of no thoughts other than our friendship."

So that night Abraham once more was delayed in one more everlasting surge of friendship and laughing. The next morning,

42

his sway-back horse, pointing west, went clopping off into the morning. Standing on the road, his legs spread wide, the great Scrimshaw waved good-bye.

"We may meet again," said Scrimshaw.

Abraham turned his head back and headed west. There were tears in his eyes. All life begins with pleasure and pain and ends with pain too. But Abraham was beginning to see that there also was pain in between every new beginning and every ending.

Several days later, Abraham stopped by the Arden plantation, to water his horse. Before long, Arden's slaves were bounding up to see the "Lazarus alive": Abraham, there in front of them.

"Goodness, Lord gracious, it's good to see you, man," said Royal Lee, "we thought y'all was dead. But here you are riding a big old swayback horse. What's ya doin'?"

"I'm going back to get something," said Abraham.

"We know what should be with you! Must be that Sarah girl at the Turner plantation."

"Must be," said Abraham. "Listen, boys, what 'come of her?"

"She's still waitin' fur ya, and she'll wait for you fur ever, too, but you better hurry up now, because word is spreading so fast across these plantations, that she'll know you're there before you're there!" They laughed and so did Abraham.

He got back up on his horse and rode on. His heart pounding, racing, and hoping that she'd be there.

Of course, word did spread fast. Like wildfire. Sarah was in the kitchen when she heard. "Abraham's comin'! Abraham's comin'!" said Emily. "Girl, you better clean yurself up and go find that man before some other girl snatches him up. He's ridin' a horse, you know!"

Sarah was breathless, running around, trying to figure what she should do. She ran to the shack where she lived with her sister and mother, and did as best she could to fix herself up. Her mother said, "Sarah, don't be too anxious with that man, now. You don't know where he's been and what he's done."

"Oh, mama," said Sarah, "he's come back for me and you know it."

"I don't know nuthin', 'cept the fact that every man is a man and men are men. Y'all be careful."

Of course, Sarah didn't care what her mother said. She ran to the edge of the plantation as fast as her bare feet could move her. As the sun was setting in the afternoon sky, she saw her man up on his horse. He stopped in the middle of the road and looked to her.

"Lord, but I don't know if that's an angel from heaven above, or my Sarah," said Abraham getting off his horse slowly. Sarah put her finger on her chin and looked up, "You know, I remember a man. Looked kinda like you, but he's been gone now some two years, no writing, jest a word from a house girl, and me now twenty-two. You must be his ghost!" she said laughing. "A ghost it is. A great black ghost comin' on a sway-back old horse. What's you lookin' for?"

"I see what I'm lookin' for," Abraham said, "If she'll have me."

They walked closer, then closer still, but did not touch. He gazed into her brown eyes and she looked at him with compassion, and awe, and then both with a smiling satisfaction that says sometimes waiting is worth the wait.

They hugged and embraced tightly, really tightly, for the first time, not feeling awkward like they had before when they had promised each other to themselves. They hugged tighter still when they felt the warmth of each other, and laughed and giggled, dizzy from the feeling of their own love.

'Course they laid together that night. There was no ceremony, but they were together as God Almighty intended man and woman to be. The next morning, just like you'd think, Turner came.

"Are you with my Sarah girl?" said Turner.

"You know, Mr. Turner, I love Sarah. I want her to be my wife."

"Then you'll have to stay here," said Turner, "for she's my mistress' helper, not yours."

"I won't steal her, Master Turner, but I will pay for her."

"She's a mighty fine woman, I don't think I'll sell her."

"Would you sell her for the money that I have here?" said Abraham. "It's $800 more than you would need to buy two women as good as Sarah at an auction block. More than the cost of a boy buck to plow your fields or break your horses."

Turner laughed, "I won't sell her." Turner's fat belly jiggled as he said this.

The tables had turned for Turner now. For the only time in many years, Turner had something Abraham wanted. Once before, Abraham had bargained a hard deal, now Abraham knew that Turner had him.

"Master Turner," Abraham said in his most earnest voice, "there are few things that you can do to break me, but that woman, I need her and she need me. Can you see it in your heart, sir, let me buy her fair and square. I cannot live without her, she is my air and my water, sure enough without her, I'll die."

"My, my, Abraham", said Turner, "your traveling turned you into something of a poet, boy. I'll tell you what I'll do. You give me your money, and, ah . . . what you got there in that sack there, son?" said Turner sarcastically. Folks didn't like him for freeing this slave, despite his woes, and needs. But, like always, Turner needed more money. Course Turner always needed money. He was gonna take the money, but was squeezing Abraham for every dollar he could.

"Why, this is, ah, . . . a brooch, sir."

"Let me see it."

You know, I think my wife Abbey would love that. So you give me that and your money, and that woman, Sarah, will be yours. Turner stood triumphantly, thinking he'd took everything he could.

Abraham had given up so much and now he had to give up what he wanted to give to his woman, but he had to do it. And so, his Sarah's broach was Miss Abbey's broach, and Turner's slave became Abraham's wife.

Chapter VIII

The Way North

Abraham and Sarah's wedding day came and the whole plantation of slaves celebrated, out of sight of the Turners and the other whites. The fiddle playing that Abraham displayed that day was quite fine, what with him having a little of the style taught by the Englishman and his own quick fingers practicing at sea for so long. The whole party was dancing to the reels and jigs he'd learned from Mobley. Yes, he had practiced for hours in the open ocean, and it showed. "You surprise me everyday," remarked Sarah, "Next you'll tell me you got a mansion out in Charlotte we'll be moving too," she shouted. The women around her were hand-in-hand reeled in a circle, Abraham and the other players banged out their songs. Abraham yelled back, "For you, my Sarah, if I could, I would, but you already cost me a fortune and we've not yet even shared a child together," he crooned. "You love as good as you fiddle, and that will come soon enough," she yelled back to him. She laughed so hard as she said this, she lost her hand with the other girls, and Abraham lost tempo with the tune.

There was a custom in the community, all gave what they could to the newlyweds. Sparse as the situation was, a plate here, a spoon, a coarse blanket. The giving came without expectation beyond wishing well to the two. For all knew that Abraham and Sarah would soon be gone. Unlike so many others, though, in past years, they weren't stolen away, weren't

47

sold, weren't yanked from their mother, weren't no child stolen from a father. They knew that Abraham was going north with his Sarah, to a better place.

So did Ike Clemmer. On the night before their sunrise leaving, Clemmer stopped by Abraham and Sarah's shed. The shed had been vacated by big George for the newlyweds as a gift. A knock on the door brought Abraham jumping to his feet, his neck was a tingle, the kind you get when your instincts is calling out "danger".

"It's time for you to leave," slathered Clemmer, clearly drunk. Abraham immediately sized up the situation. Clemmer, his courage fortified with drink, was not about to back down as he had done before.

"Ike Clemmer," said Abraham, saying his full name so as to alert the half-sleeping Sarah of the urgency of the situation. "I am leaving on the morrow and won't come to this here place no more. You, I sure, will be happy with this," soothed Abraham.

"You will do what I say now, negra, and pick up that wench and leave, before we take and whip y'all. Now get, both ya."

For the first time, Abraham's focus was no longer directed at Ike, but behind him, and the look brought a shudder. For behind Ike there were shadows and in the shadows five mean white men with clubs and torches immediately stood out in the evening. They all seemed to have the same feeling toward him and his new bride. Abraham knew that this was not the time to fight, but to get moving, quick as possible.

"Sarah," Abraham whispered out of the side of his mouth, "pack up your stuff, woman, now! We gotta leave."

"Mister Ike," Abraham said, "I can't get ready that fast, we'll be gone early sunrise tomorrow if you just wait. You see, I still got my horse and the cart and they aren't hitched yet, so, ah, if ya . . ."

"Go on, get it done now, before I lose my temper and sic these fellas on ya now," screamed Clemmer.

"Why are you so against me," plead Abraham, hoping a logical question would help.

"I don't like no self-freed negras! Don't want 'um, don't need 'um. Spoil everythin', and throw the other negras into some kind of attitude.

Abraham knew he couldn't fight this evil logic. The whole south stunk by the injustice of humans owning other humans. But there he stood, the exception.

You know even back in old ancient Rome them slaves could earn their freedom. Yes sir, even in this country of America, only 100 years before Abraham's mother was born, negroes could work to earn freedom, or could get free by becoming Christians. But it all changed. The noose so bad that you were condemned to it at birth: condemned by your skin, condemned by who you were. Unless, of course, you ran or outsmarted them. Abraham had done better than most. He had worked and bargained for his freedom. For them Ike Clemmers, though, Abraham was bad.

Ike fingered his belt, and in the dark of a dull crescent moon, Abraham could see a gun. Abraham nodded, "I'll gather my things now, sir. Sarah and I be gone. Give me time to harness the horse and get my wagon and get my mama."

Abraham shut the door behind him and he heard Sarah put the latch on the lock. There he stood alone with Sarah in the half darkness, now lit by a single candle. Sarah was trembling. Abraham was hoping to distract the men towards him and not his bride.

"Walk with me, Ike, ah, while I go and hitch Bess."

Abraham hoped to take the group as far away from his Sarah as possible. Sarah's stomach was convulsing in fear. She quickly gathered what she could, now not caring what wedding gifts were left behind. "Please, please," she said, "God don't let them kill him."

Before, Sarah had no use for no God. Never plead His name, never prayed like the others. She never prayed for a God she thought would allow humans to do what had been done to her and hers. She didn't pray for her salvation and she didn't pray for something other than what she could get here on earth. God let her be a slave, but only Abraham was helping get her free. Often times her mama would say, "Stop the blasphemy, girl, don't you say that God don't exist." So Sarah would keep to herself about it, but she wasn't repenting. Not by no means at all. She'd tell her friends, "There is no God for us, only death or stolen freedom. Only freedom most gits is with death."

But now Sarah had something to lose, now. It was her man, Abraham, who was in mortal danger and Sarah invoked the name of God for him, her man, but not for herself.

Within ten minutes, all that was to go with her for her new life was in three bundles in a pile at the foot of the door of the shack. Abraham still did not return. Another ten minutes passed with no sound nor word.

Finally, after what Sarah thought was a lifetime of waiting in fear, there came a knock softly at the door. "Sarah!" whispered Abraham. "We gots to go now!"

When she opened the door wide, the torches illuminated the night, five in all, all held by the white men surrounding Abraham's old humble cart. Sitting atop the carriage was Abraham's mother, Reena. She was half asleep, but scared to death and frozen in fear.

"Come, now," Abraham plead. The surrounding men came closer to him. Sarah launched her bundles, all three, into the wagon and sprang aboard. With a false cheeriness she said to Abraham, "Time to go, Abraham." She shouted out loud, "Good-bye to y'all, Mr. Clemmer, we ain't goin' to see you again," hoping her confidence would stop any evil of Clemmer and the others.

Abraham sprang onto the wagon and turned Bess and the wagon around. Abraham said to Clemmer, "We'll be going now. Good night and good-bye." He took the reins, hissed and Bess began slowly clippity-clopping off the property. But the torches and Clemmer followed them. When they got to the edge of the property, off of the Turner plantation and onto the road, Ike spurred his horse and stopped the old horse in its track. Clemmer said, "You think this is still gonna end now? Y'all ain't paid me yet."

Abraham was surprised. "Paid you for what?" asked Abraham. "For letting us leave? Please, Mr. Clemmer, we don't want no trouble. Leave us be, please?"

Clemmer retorted, "Why y'all leaving with a slave of Mister Turner's. Sure enough, your mama, and that ain't right, and the negro girl, Sarah, is master's, not yours."

Abraham barely understood the intoxicated spitting of of Ike's talk. "Now, sir," Abraham said, "you know I got a Bill of Sale for Sarah and mama's blind. She ain't no good for no one. Please, now, let us pass."

"No!" Shouted Ike, "you ain't going 'til I say and now you payin'."

Ike was reaching for his holster and the gleaming handle of his pistol and Abraham was pleading, "I ain't got no money, sir, I got nothin' for you, please, sir, let us pass."

The torches illuminated a circle in the night. But in the edges of that darkness stood a horse and a rider. As all the white men looked only at Ike and Abraham, nobody could see him. But just as Ike reached for his pistol, there was a sudden gun flash, and a boom in the night. Ike Clemmer flopped off his horse, like a slice off a roast beef from a sharp knife. He hit the ground and groaned and his horse ran off.

Suddenly the horse and the man in the dark came closer. The man had a pistol in each hand and as he came up, he glared at the other white men who had gone to the aid of Ike and were directly in line of his pistol fire. The huge man roared at the white men, "Who comes to stop me and mine? Who dare to stop my vision I seen in the bones. Who come to take not what is his?"

The white men looked frozen as they stared at the big black man who spoke so strange.

The torches outlined his figure, as he sat there in his cloak like a black tornado on a large horse. It was Scrimshaw, his pistols pointed directly at them, and them whites knew that their day was numbered if they didn't abide his words.

"You be gone, now," he said to the men as he pointed the pistols, and off they ran like cockroaches hiding to the light of day about to be slapped by a giant hand.

Abraham was numb, he couldn't believe his eyes. He sat there on the running board with his mouth opened, being unable to say anything at all, but hearing his mama say, "Who, who is that Gabriel come blowin' trumpets in the night? Who is that? Who is that?"

When Reena said this, Sarah roared in laughter, probably more just to release the tension of the moment than the funniness of what Reena was saying.

"I'm no Gabriel, woman!" said Scrimshaw. "I'm Scrimshaw of the seven seas. I'm Abraham's friend, just come to see him off. Come to see that me bones come true."

He looked at Abraham directly. "You listen to me, Abraham. You be gone, man, like the wind. Take your women and leave. Hurry. I'll chase 'em as far as I can, then turn and ride toward Charleston." He raised his hands with his pistols and in a gesture of farewell said, "This was meant to be, you and me. That's what I couldn't tell you in the bones. I'm glad I could see why you came back for your Sarah. She is a very beautiful woman."

With that, Sarah blushed in the darkness, embarrassed by his compliment. "Now hurry. If you don't go soon, I'll take her for myself." Scrimshaw roared with laughter. Then he pointed his pistols north and said, "Be gone."

Abraham couldn't say nothing until, as he turned the old horse north, he yelled back, "Scrimshaw!" But by then, the great man was galloping his horse towards them running white men, pistols cocked. Abraham never did see him again.

Chapter IX

New Orleans

Abraham knew that Scrimshaw could only keep off them baying hounds of Ike Clemmer and his gang for a short period of time. Besides, old Bessie took her load as fast as she could, so Abraham had to take a turn to the West.

"We should be headin' North," Sarah pleaded to Abraham.

"No, we can't. Clemmer is gonna have every paddy-roller looking for us as run-away slaves just to stop us. Those slave catchers will look for us headin' North, not West," said Abraham sternly.

Sarah was too frightened to argue.

"Listen, Sarah, we will only travel at night for a few weeks. When we get to the Alabama river, were gonna be goin' South again. I'm gonna go west to New Orleans. I know, I know that the place that we are lookin' for is gonna be up the Mississippi River. That's the only big river that I think we can find a place away from all them Clemmers of the world."

For weeks they followed this pattern, traveling at night, placing themselves out of harm's way. It was always this way when you was on the run. You could get aid from other negroes on plantations. They'd spare food, and when he could, Abraham would do labor.

Reena would ask almost every evening, "Tell me, son, about that big man with his scars."

"Oh, now, Mama Reena, please!" said Sarah most disgusted, "We beat that wash clean a long time ago. Stop askin'."

"Sush, now Sarah," Reena would say. "Let me hear that story. Abraham tells it so good."

Almost as a nightly ritual, Abraham would, of course, tell the story of his great friend Scrimshaw and all their adventures together.

Being skilled, Abraham often did find work in towns along the way. When they finally got to the mouth of the Alabama River, they went further south to the Mobile River. There, Abraham met a fisherman by the name of Burrows, who was taking his catch to New Orleans. In exchange for his labor, Burrows agreed to take them with him.

"Ya, know," said Burrows in a deep bass voice, "New Orleans is a bon temps place for you. Yep, plenty of Negroes there, but mostly slaves getting sold."

Abraham had heard of the selling that was going on at the time.

"Yes, I hear," Abraham said. "A lot more slaves needed now for them cotton plantations. The English pay a good price for the cotton, don't they?" said Abraham in a dry voice he used when talkin' to whites about slavery.

"That they do. That they do," said Burrows, "Now help me with these here nets and let's get to workin'."

The journey was not a good one for Sarah.

"Sarah? Have you stopped throwin' up yet?" said Reena, as they rocked heavily in the Gulf waters along the Mississippi sound.

"I'm never, ever, gettin' in a boat again!" chimed Sarah, "Never!"

Eventually Sarah's stomach settled in and she and Reena spent most of their days trying to avoid the fishy smell and

Sarah looking along the distant shores for any interesting sights.

When they had finally gotten off Burrows' boat, and Abraham had helped unload the cargo, the whole family started investigating the market. There was a wonderful collection of people and goods.

Sarah had never seen such a large city with so many Negroes mixing with white, mixing with other folk.

Abraham got lodging at a small rooming house and went about seeing where he might find some work. In a small saloon called the King Louis, he walked up to the bar to order something to satisfy a thirst created by that hot Louisiana sun. Standing at the bar next to him, was a tall, thin man dressed in a suit. He was a light skinned Negro and Abraham noticed his hair was slicked back and in wavy rows and he had a tall hat in his left hand. As he was picking up his drink, the man spoke to him.

"W. P. Wilkins is my name, good man. Who is you?"

"My name is Abraham Cooper. Pleased to meet you."

"You're new here," Wilkins intoned.

"Yes. I'm headin' up north, up the Mississippi," said Abraham.

"Well, this is a great town to be in, if you're gonna stay. Great city, New Orleans," Wilkins said, "But a powerful expensive one."

"I have very little money," Abraham said.

"What Negro does?" said Wilkins. "I myself have little. But these clothes I'm wearin' is French. They are fancy, are they not?"

"Yes, they are," said Abraham. And at that, Abraham heard the full story of Mr. W.P. Wilkins. French mother, negro father. Fur trapping uncle, whom Wilkins himself wanted to join up

56

along the Missouri River.

After a month of working at docks and of nightly conversations with Mr. Wilkins, Abraham and W.P. started discussing the river.

"You know who Lewis & Clark is, don't ya?" asked Wilkins. "Well, they say that along the Missouri there is a great fertile plain with plenty of game and fur tradin' posts are already up there. And they could use men like us."

"I know that what I'm lookin' for," replied Abraham, "is land to farm."

"Well, y'all got to go," Wilkins suggested, "before the whites take all the good land."

"Missouri is a slave state now! Abraham spat back. "I ain't goin' there."

"Then try the Illinois side, that's free."

Later that week, Abraham was able to purchase steerage passage on a keel boat and Wilkins did, too. And so they traveled up the great Mississippi River, just as Scrimshaw's bones foretold. Wilkins took quite a liking to Sarah and he would often speak to her in French. But after several days of keel boating north, Sarah said she weren't feeling so good, so they had to stop and rest in St. Louis.

Chapter X

A Free Son

One night, sitting before the fire of their camp outside of St. Louis, Sarah kneeled down in front of Abraham. "Hold me tight," she said in her sweetest voice.

They held each other close as the flames slowly flickered in the fire and made little shadows on their faces.

"You know, when I look up at the stars, I ask myself why God put us here," Sarah said. "Just slavery and suffering until you come along. I didn't even want to believe in no God, but the man I see that's you, with your dreams and how much you've done and how much you love me, I guess there is a reason."

Abraham jumped in putting his hands on each side of her face, "I'm here to love you," he said, "That's why God put me here."

Sarah looked in his eyes. "Could you love another?" she asked.

"Another woman? No, no, no," exclaimed Abraham in a high pitched voice.

She laughed, "Not another woman. A baby, Abraham. I'm havin' your baby!"

Abraham fell back on his heels and shouted out to the sky, "Lord, thank you God, you havin' a baby!"

"Be quiet, now," Sarah said, "or you'll wake Reena. I haven't told her yet. I do need to rest and stay here for awhile," said Sarah.

"Why, we'll move here for good, if need be," said Abraham.

"No, we won't," Sarah said resolutely, "We're gonna find your land and we're gonna farm it and we're gonna raise our children, just like your dream. But until such time as this child come, we'll work and save our money. Don't give up your dream, Abraham. Scrimshaw's bones, they don't lie. We'll get up there and get that land.

Samuel Cooper was born that winter. W.P. helped Abraham carve the initials "S.C." and "1824" on his fiddle. Abraham worked at a tanner's. Reena sewed. But the good came with the bad and Wilkins caught some kinda fever and was very sick come early 1825.

Abraham stood over the coughing, ashen-faced Wilkins.

"W.P., how ya feelin'?" he asked in a solemn tone.

"I'm getting better, I'm getting stronger every day," W.P. said. "I think, though, I'm gonna need some help getting on the *Belle Rose* if we're gonna take her up north."

Abraham had gotten hired on to work on the *Belle Rose*, which was heading up the Mississippi.

"Can't say for sure how much I can help," W.P. said, "But I'll . . . I'll . . ." He tried to lift himself on his elbows as he said this, but he coughed and fell back.

"I can't wait much longer. The *Belle Rose* is leaving in two days," said Abraham to Sarah that night. "Do we leave W.P. behind?"

Sarah was rocking Samuel in her arms when she said, "Not the Abraham I know. He ain't never left no one behind. We'll just have to wait until W.P. gets better."

And so they waited for W.P. to improve, but by April, it was clear that he was not getting better.

One evening Abraham was standing next to the bed when

W.P. asked him to come closer so they could talk. W.P., in his weak voice, said "You know I told you about my Uncle, Rene DeRussey? He has a trading post up along the Missouri. By steam boat it won't take long to get there. I want to see him again before I die. I know I can make it if you help me. I know it would take you out of your way, but I'd be forevermore in your debt if you did so."

W.P. looked up at Abraham with cloudy eyes, and Abraham knew that what he was watching was a dying man's request.

"You sure you can make it?" said Abraham. "It will be awful difficult movin' you and all."

"If I'm gonna die," said W.P., "I'd rather be with my uncle, the only family I got left, than here, in St. Louis."

"Well, you rest easy tonight," said Abraham to W.P. "We'll take care of that tomorrow.

The next morning, while they were cooking the morning meal, Abraham told Sarah about W.P.

"Abraham, he's probably gonna die on the trip, you know that."

"I know, Sarah, but when a man looks you in the eye with a dying request and you're his friend, you do what you can."

"I know," Sarah said, "Sometimes I just wish that you was the type of man that would think first of himself, instead of always thinking of others. But you ain't, so if you have to go, God's speed, but come back quickly. Samuel be missin' ya already."

Before he left, he held Samuel in his arms and he played the fiddle some and that made the boy smile. Then he and another man helped W.P. down to the docks where they caught the *Independence* heading up the Missouri river.

As the steamboat headed north, she suddenly veered west,

for here, St. Louis breaks the Mississippi River up. Straight north, you're up the Mississippi to Minnesota. But heading west, and you're along the Missouri River. Much to Abraham's surprise, the landscape of Missouri was breathtaking. The land was lush along the river bluffs and not many people.

With what strength he had, W.P. talked about his uncle, Rene DeRussey.

"DeRussey is one of them old-time fur trappers. A Frenchman as big as a bear and a deep laugh. You'll find him at Boone's Lick where he's got a trading post and some land that he's holding to, although he can't farm worth a darn. It was Rene that kept me and mama in venison when we were in hard scrabble in New Orleans.

W.P. coughed some after he finished talking. To make more light of the situation, Abraham said, "Sounds to me like your family is close."

"Oh, yes," W.P. said, "very."

"You know what my mama would call that?" Abraham asked, "She would say good family is as close as a lean tick to a sick kitten."

W.P. laughed, "What's that mean".

"I'm not really sure," Abraham said, "But it always sounded funny when mama would say it.

The steamboat was filled with goods and people going north. The river was all about trading for fur and such. Some of the men on the boat weren't wearin' no store-bought clothes. They were in buckskin that made Abraham think that he was finally heading towards the real frontier.

On the fifth day, Abraham got up, and as was his custom on board, went to get some water and food for W.P., but it was of no use. W.P. had died in the night, resting comfortably on the floor in blankets. Abraham thought it a shame that W.P. would never get to see or hold the hand of his uncle again in this life.

Being as they were close to their destination, Abraham rolled up his friend tightly in the blankets and bound him and said little to the captain or passengers, except nodding that W.P. was still not feeling too well, but did not let them know of his passing.

When the ferry docked at Boone's Lick, Abraham looked up to see nothing but a wooden plank leading from shore and a small bunch of buildings up on a bluff. By this time, he had let the captain know of W.P.'s death, and seeing as W.P. didn't have no catchable diseases, two of the crew helped Abraham bring the body off.

Abraham saw an old woman sitting there and asked where he might find Rene DeRussey. The toothless lady, smoking a pipe, pointed up towards a building and said nothing further. When he got up to the building and knocked on the door, he heard a loud voice heavily accented French saying, "Who dare? Come in then!"

"Are you Rene DeRussey? I am a friend of your nephew's," said Abraham.

W.P. was right about one thing, Abraham thought. This was a giant of a man in buckskin and he must have weighed over 300 pounds.

"You come to talk to me 'bout my nephew?" Rene said.

"I brought him up with me."

At that, the Frenchman spun his head.

"Where is he?"

"He got sick outside St. Louis, and passed just this day ago on board the riverboat," Abraham said sadly.

At that, the great man's eyes teared up, and as his chin quivered, he stepped out into the open air. Rene carried W.P. by himself up to a bluff overlooking the river. He and Abraham buried him there. Rene recited a prayer in French, and Abraham picked up his fiddle and played a tune achingly good.

"It was W.P.'s favorite song," Abraham said to Rene, "I often played it for him. You know, all he talked about was how much he wanted to come here and be with you."

"That would have been something, eh!," Rene said, "I thank you for your friendship to him. There are many good men up here. I see that you, too, are one, because you, you honored your friend's request. "Have you been up here before, Abraham?"

"No, but it is beautiful."

"This is a good land. Since the government opened it up, many people come out west. They are the new Americans, my nephew's friend. Once there was more freedom here than anywhere else, but now those 'merdes' bring their slavery here. Do you know why the revolution against the British was lost?"

"Lost?" said Abraham, "It weren't lost."

"Yes, it was, my friend. I am a Frenchman, I know. No people can be free unless all people are free. You know more than me, all are not."

"Yes, I do," Abraham said, "Yes, I do."

That night, Rene and Abraham went back down to a small cabin and ate wild venison and drank whiskey. Renee sang French songs and Abraham played his fiddle.

Chapter XI

The Great River

A braham loved the land around the upper Missouri River. The low cliffs were sometimes white above the river and green carpets of grass stood above them. In as much as he wished to be a good guest to Rene, he knew he needed to leave as quickly as possible to get back to Sarah and Samuel.

"Rene, when does the next steamboat come going south?"

Rene thought a moment. "It could be a week, it could be maybe ten days," said Rene.

"That's too long," said Abraham. "Then I gotta catch a keelboat heading south. There must be trappers heading towards St. Louis?"

"I would not trust them to get you there safely," said Rene. "It is safer to wait for the riverboat. Don't be sad. I will show you a good time. Today we go hunting," said Rene.

Rene handed Abraham a long flintlock rifle and soon he and the big Frenchman were traveling up the banks of the Missouri River on horseback. Except for the small trading post, there were no people. When they got to a bluff, Rene pointed across the river.

"There, do you see that point there? That is the land I own."

Across the river Abraham saw a small sandy beach area and a sloping bank which led to a gently sloping plain where a creek must have been running as trees were dotted in a line like a great green path between the grasses. Abraham's jaw dropped in disbelief.

"This is yours?"

"Of course," Rene said. "The government is selling grants of land and I bought 300 acres right over there."

Abraham looked at Rene, "It's as if a painting had been in my mind and now is alive in front of me," said Abraham. "This is what I saw in my head."

Rene and Abraham camped that night along the river eating the quail that Rene had shot. Abraham told Rene the whole story of the bones Scrimshaw threw for him and his dream of a farm. Around that fire, Rene agreed to sell his land to Abraham. Abraham could not believe his great fortune as having finally found the land that he knew in his mind must exist.

"It is crazy for sure," Abraham said, "that I come up this river for a dying man's wish, and find the land for my home."

"Life turns in strange ways," Rene said, "sometimes when you seem to go one way, it brings you another. I will wait for you and your family to come back, and will expect you to have some money for the down payment when you return."

The next day, Abraham ferried across the river and spent the next two days riding with Rene along the floor of the valley laying out in his mind's eye where he would put his house and where he'd set his barn and where he'd put his corral.

When they returned to the trading post, Rene and Abraham signed an agreement for the sale. Until the river boat arrived, Abraham was like a boy waiting for Christmas morning to come.

Chapter XII

The Farmin' Kind

When Abraham returned to St. Louis, he told Sarah of the land.

"Abraham, I thought we were goin' to a free state. I thought we were leavin' the slave country."

"I know," said Abraham, "but this land is for us. I saw it in my mind. There is hardly anyone up in the area. Just a small town up north and Rene says that there some farmers close by, even two, three negro families."

"Abraham, I followed you this far. I suppose I'll have to follow you to this dream place, but are you sure?"

"I hate the idea of living with slave farmers, but there are free farmers up there, too. Sarah, believe in me, woman."

She sighed, "I do, I do."

So they went north, took the Independence the next month and started their life on Abraham's land, along the Missouri River.

By the end of 1825, Abraham had constructed a house from the willow trees which ran by the creek on his property and he and Sarah, spent 12 and 14 hour days, slowly cutting and carving a garden of corn, wheat and squash. Rene would visit frequently, especially in the first winter. Abraham even constructed his own small work area at the trading post and was paid pretty good wage to fix broken things that the folks heading further along the Santa Fe Trail needed repairin'.

They were often visited by Nelson and Ella Thompson, a Negro couple from a little ways west, who had owned their land since before Missouri had become a state. Nelson had been freed by his "massa" as he used to say, as a dying man's thank you, and purchased his wife, Ella, from the massa's son. Ella, Reena and Sarah had their own little "talk sessions," as Abraham would like to tease Sarah. Ella herself was childless, and therefore, was always making inquiry about when Sarah would have another.

"Sure, woman, you should have at least enough children to help on this farm of yours," Ella would ask. "When is your next one coming?"

Sarah would laugh. "I guess when the good Lord bring it," she would say.

And Ella would say, "Well you better get that man of yours working on it. From what I can tell, he works so hard on this farm and by the end of the day, he could sleep on a nail."

"Oh, we find the time. Don't you worry about that," said Sarah.

One evening after finishing their harvest of 1827, Sarah found Abraham in the field as the light of the day was fading. It was humid and warm. Abraham was sweaty from his labor. Sarah whispered in his ear, "You know how much I love you?" Abraham held her and right there they laid in that field as a man and a woman do, in their field, their farm. They stayed until the darkness came. When they returned, a worried Reena was asking why they was walking in the dark like that. At which the two giggled and laughed at one another like two small children caught with their hand in the cookie jar.

Chapter XIII

Stolen

L ittle William come to the world in June, 1828. When the baby's namin' occurred, there was a whole pile of people on Abraham's land celebratin'. The Thompsons were there, as was Mars Bolling, who Abraham said looked like a big round yellow ball 'cause his beard and hair was of yellow straw color. A negro name of Raw Stevens was there. He was a trapper and fur trader. During the party, Stevens talked of what he had seen just west.

"Negroes better be real careful. Paddy-rollers are out. When I was out in the west territory, the Cherokee's were telling me that the paddy-rollers are looking for runaway slaves and even going as far as paying for Cherokee's slaves to bring back for bounty."

Abraham spit onto the ground. "Is there anything more low-life than a bounty-hunting man trying to chain a man's freedom."

"Well, you just keep a sharp eye. I heard that they were heading back down the Missouri, and a man can never be too careful, even if you are a free Negro," said Stevens looking at Abraham.

"Well, don't scare the women, unless you have to," said Nelson, "but we'll keep a sharp lookout."

By this time, Abraham's labor had brought him three horses. He was going to the trading post riding his horse, Ben, with

Angel and Nina, his pack horses. It was fall and he wanted to trade before the winter. The creek on his land emptied into the river, and on an afternoon when the moths were flying in great clouds around the trees, Abraham bent down to get some water. His horses were also quenching their thirst in the wash-out.

He said out loud, for no particular reason, to himself, "Lord, but what a day this is." Behind him he heard the breaking of branches, and suddenly felt a large shoe kick him in the side of the head.

"We sure snuck up on that stupid nigger," said Ed Watson to his bossman, John Libbing. "Quick, now, tie up them horses with the others and chain that nigger to that wagon."

As they dragged Abraham, he groaned mightily and tried to stand up, and was again kicked by Watson. He was thrown in the wagon and chained to two others, but at the time, could neither see nor hear what had happened.

It was the paddy-rollers come to take slaves back for the bounty on their heads. Most didn't care if a man were free or not, if somebody would pay for them. John Libbing was just such a man. He wore a broad brimmed hat and a buffalo hide vest and stank from his own smell. The man probably never bathed more than once in his 30 odd years. Like a head rat with smaller mice servants, Watson and Boyle did what Libbing told them to do.

The horses were tied up behind the wagon and the whole group headed down to the ferry to cross the river. Where Abraham bent over to drink water in the creek lay Abraham's "free papers". They'd all fallen out when he was hit and dragged on the ground. The very papers Mr. Stein told him to always keep. Now he had no proof he was a free man. But Abraham didn't know it yet.

A few hours later, Abraham's head was pounding and he

69

shook himself to clear it. He lifted his head up and was sitting in a wagon. Next to him were two other Negroes. He moved some and could feel irons on his hands and rope around his legs. Abraham looked at the bald headed negro next to him.

"Who's the boss here."

The Negro replied, "The buffalo man standing there near the ferryman."

There standing on the ferry was the paddy-roller, John Libbing. Yes, they were taking the ferry to the east side of the Missouri. Abraham knew he would soon be sold back into slavery if he couldn't get out of the mess he was in. The wagon and the horses were in the middle of the river when he stood up and called out.

"Mister, there is a mistake here. You must a thought I was a runaway or something, but I'm not. I'm free and I got papers to prove it."

Libbing turned his cold face toward Abraham.

"You sit down and be quiet or I'll gag your mouth," he said.

"But sir, I'm free. Let me show you."

Abraham was reaching into his pocket for his papers, but try as he might, he couldn't find them. He kept slapping his hands over himself searching to each pocket, but still the papers weren't there.

"Sir, I must have left them back at my cabin, on my farm. You see, I've got a farm, and . . ."

"Shut up and sit down, Nigger," said Watson who had walked over.

The bald Negro said to Abraham, "You better sit down or they'll whip ya."

"But I'm a free man. Free. Do you hear me?" Abraham kept talking louder and louder, finally shouting, "Let me go, I tell ya

I'm free."

At that point, Watson swung with the butt of his rifle, but as the river was moving and rocking, instead of hitting him in the stomach, Abraham took the butt of the rifle in his cheek. You could hear the "crack" of something breaking.

A flash of heat and rage went over Abraham and he jumped on Watson. They both tumbled out of the wagon together and fell onto the floor of the barge and then rolled into the water. The weight of them falling in pushed the bald headed Negro off the wagon and he was holding on for dear life.

Struggling in the water together, Abraham wrapped his chains around Watson's neck.

But the current was strong and they were both driven under the ferry. Libbing was trying to pull Watson back in, and Boyle was trying to keep the other Negro from falling into the river.

"Boyle," screamed Libbing, "cut the leg rope or we'll lose all of them to the river."

Boyle did as he was told and the rope fell into the water. Watson and Abraham went under together as one man with four arms and four legs.

"Do you see them?"

"No, I don't!" said a disgusted Libbing. "That river must of got them both. Damn, Watson was a good man, too."

"The bodies will float downstream," said Libbing dully and turned. He hustled with Boyle to put the bald man back in the wagon.

In the water, the struggle ended with Watson's grip on Abraham finally loosening. Abraham had been able to take a breath before being pulled under the ferry, but he couldn't remember getting thrown by the current, away from Watson's body. The current pushed him to an eddy on the western bank, but he wasn't conscious of anything for a long, long time.

71

Chapter XIV

The Lost Man

On days when Abraham was going to the trading post, Sarah would get up and fix him a big breakfast of corn pone and honey.

"You give your children a kiss good-bye?" she said.

"Yes, ma'am, I did. And I'll give you a kiss, too."

Abraham bent over from his horse to kiss Sarah good-bye. But Sarah turned her cheek to him. She was mad at him because there was work to be done here at the farm. Yet he had promised Rene that he would go down to work on a couple of wagon axles that needed to be repaired and Abraham had corn to trade, too.

"Listen, Sarah, we could use the money and the farm work can wait for a few days. I'll be back to help you, just wait."

Two days passed, but Sarah did not think about her last kiss to her man. After a week, she got concerned. And then, she heard word.

"It seems that the ferryman recognized Abraham as he stood up. But before anything could be said, Abraham plunged into the river with the white paddy-roller," said Rene.

Sarah collapsed. Moaning, crying, "Did you find his body?" she sobbed.

"Nothing, Sarah, he might still be alive. He a strong man."

Mama Reena screamed out when she heard.

"Oh, Lord, oh, Lord, is there no end to this? Can't they just leave us be. Please God almighty."

Willy was crying for food and Samuel, who was just starting to talk, knew something was up, and was asking why mama was crying.

Rene said, "I also found papers by the creek. Here," he said, and gave them to Sarah.

Sarah knew instantly what they were and clasped them to her bosom, but she could not speak a word. Now she was by herself, Sarah thought, and two children and a blind mama.

Reena and Sarah sat down that evening after Samuel and Willie were asleep.

"We got to find out what happened," said Reena, "Make them pay for killing my Abraham."

"I can't think about that right now, Mama Reena," Sarah said. "I wish I could, but I can't. I've got too much to do to keep us together here!"

At that, she buried her head in Reena's arms.

Chapter XV

The Farm Woman

There's some who withers and shrink from hard times and there's others that grit and set their jaws and overcome it. Sarah wailed over her man loudly at first, but thereafter, did so quietly and alone.

Two days following Rene's telling her about what had happened to Abraham, she vowed to stay and work the land. Her land, with her children, just as Abraham had dreamed that they would do. Sarah had become a farmer and she liked the life. Before she had been a house cook, not toiling on the land like other Negroes. Abraham, though he liked the farm life, wasn't the farmer that she was. Sarah had the knack for growing things that Abraham did not. Abraham brought her here, but it was Sarah that made herself the farmer she'd become.

The paddy-rollers took their two horses, but Sarah plowed under the field for winter with her bay horse, Judy. William got a fever, but Reena boiled Jerusalem root and gave him a tea for a week that cured him. Still, it was all Sarah; Sarah the farmer, the mother and the father. Sarah who took care of all as best that she could.

Reena helped as she could and the Thompsons would go to the trading post for her and some of Reena's work made money too.

The Thompsons were the best of neighbors and would come

often with food, and as winter approached, even asked Sarah if she wanted to stay with them.

"No," said Sarah, "I'll stay here. This is my farm. What if Abraham comes back? He would want us to be here."

At that, Ella Thompson looked at her husband in silence, then looked back. Finally she said to Sarah, "You know, Sarah, it's time to give him his blessing and send him on his way. Let Gabriel's horn blow him home."

"I will not!" Sarah shouted, "Not yet. I won't give up."

Riding in their carriage home, Ellie said to Nelson, "My, but that Sarah will not give up on her man, will she."

"Only one Lazarus I know of," replied Nelson.

Still, that night Sarah said a prayer, "God, keep my man safe, or let him be in peace with you."

Chapter XVI

The Cherokee

Florence Comes-With-A-Feather loved to travel with her father along the Missouri. She was often bored with life in her village. Her father was John Nave who was the great trader of their tribe. Her family had been living in the middle of Missouri since the big "shake," as the Cherokee liked to call it, when the earth shook back in 1811.

John Nave would travel hundreds of miles to trade. This time, they had been coming back down the Black Water River to the Missouri, heading south. They were traveling Cherokee style with single ponies packed with goods. At 18, Florence, as everyone called her, was the youngest of the Nave children. She was also the smallest, with fine thin features on her face. Her father clearly treated her as his favorite.

Florence was standing near a gravel washout when she saw an object floating towards her. She ran into the knee-deep water to see a swollen, black faced man with chains on his wrists. "A slave," she said out loud, "Must be a runaway slave."

Florence was well aware of runaway slaves for in her own village they had runaway slaves.

She was able to pull Abraham out of the river and pounded on his back, yelling, "Osiyo, osiyo!" A blinking, choking, Abraham looked up to see a young woman whose hair was wrapped in leather. She had cuts in her earlobes and little silver trinkets shaped like stars hanging from them. He tried to speak to her, but with his broken and swollen jaw, was unable to utter a word. All he could do was make a gurgling sound.

She ran to get her father. The year before, a white had killed her brother. According to Cherokee law, she could keep the slave that she had found along the river.

Florence cried out to her father in Cherokee, "My brother's life was taken by the white. I take this slave of the white to balance my brother's loss."

Beaver's Tooth Perryman and Joe Grayson were also traveling with Florence and her father with their own skins to trade. They, too, had slaves who became part of the tribe, and one named Andrew had married a widow.

When John Nave came back to see what Florence had found, he set up a quick fire and gave Abraham sips of vinegar tea with mustard to revive him.

The next thing Abraham knew, he was strapped to a pony and was heading south east back to the Cherokee village. He was too weak to even resist, and was happy only that the Indians were careful to treat him well, feed him spooned liquids and keep him warm at night. Abraham did not know what was coming next, but he was glad just to be alive.

Chapter XVII

Aniwaya

Now Florence, she was one girl who talked. She spoke English for trading, as did many Cherokee. Abraham listened as they rode. He was lying on a blanket between two poles.

She looked back and spoke to the man with her hand on the horse's rump. Her voice low in tone, "We are the old people. My father's tribe came west as the white man took our lands. Each treaty pushed us further west".

"I live with my parents and four . . ." She stopped mid sentence. "Three brothers and sister in a house overlooking Bone Creek in Missouri.

"You know Missouri has become a state? Yet even now, my Cherokee elders are trying to make a new treaty with the white man."

Beaver Tooth spoke to Joe, "Why save the slave? She'll kill him with her talk!"

"Better him listening to her than you and I. No wonder her father rides so far ahead of us," laughed Joe. They traveled for two more weeks this way.

By the time they got to her village, Abraham was sitting up on a horse, and yet Florence never stopped talking. He saw below a village with houses built French style, with vertical logs sealed with clay.

Abraham, still unable to speak, could only nod.

Florence tended to him for weeks and another Negro by the name of Drew would come by the tent where he was placed to talk with him a while.

Drew was a runaway and hooked up with the Cherokee to keep from being caught. He was a great shooter with a rifle. He told Abraham, "Cherokee is good people, but they have their own way so be careful."

It surprised Abraham that the Indians here had English names and spoke English, but he knew little of their long history with the whites.

As far as Florence was concerned, Abraham was now part of the Nave family, even if he didn't know it yet. It was a month before he had enough strength to even walk at all.

As soon as he could, though, he told Drew, "Yesh, but hime ah pree men."

"Yes," said Drew, "you're freer now than you have ever been. John said they takin' the chain off you, but don't try and escape. Cherokee can track a man through any territory."

"Yesh," said Abraham, "ah pree man."

"You keep working," said Drew, "and you'll end up having your own cabin here with us."

Abraham shook his head. He kept trying to figure out some way to get back to Sarah. How she must be suffering. What about my boys? He knew if he waited to get his strength back, he would get an opportunity. Then, before he could do anything, winter came.

Chapter XVIII

A White Man In The Night

They call them "First Frosts," when the first winter snow hits. It came in early November. The winds howled and whistled tunes between the cracks of the cabin. Sarah, bundled up in bed, became so cold so fast that the fire couldn't keep the room warm, but it gave just a bit of warmth to her and Reena and the boys.

"Of all the things to happen this year, early snow," Sarah thought to herself.

In a middle of the night, she heard a sound like a ghost howling.

"Oh, Lord," said Reena who could hear it too. "There must be devils out there tonight."

She threw another piece of wood on the fire, but could still hear the yelling, and then slowly, but surely came the sound. It seemed closer, and then closer still. Suddenly, Sarah realized someone was pounding on her door and a man was yelling. Reena stood up when she heard it too.

"Sarah, somebody's outside."

"Go get the children," said Sarah, then she reached for the rifle and approached the door.

As Sarah came to the door, she heard, "thump, thump, thump" in rhythm. Sarah went up to the door and cocked the rifle.

"Go away," she yelled, "you go away now!"

Reena felt her way up to the door.

"Get away from there Mama Reena. Step away, now." But Reena's ears were sharper than a fox.

"Shhhh, shhh! Listen! It sounds like a man need help. In this kind of weather, I can see why. Open the door!"

Reena called out, "You there, who is you now! What's your name."

Through the wind and noise, they could only hear "Oohgen, oohgen" Reena heard faintly and then more scratching.

"He'll die out there, now Sarah," Reena said. "You keep your rifle cocked and I'll unlatch the door."

As Reena unlatched the door and the wind blew in a huge cloud of white snow, there, slumping against the door and falling through it as it opened was a white man near death. There was frost on his nose and whiskers and Sarah jumped back as he fell to the floor in a cold, stiff manner.

Reena bent over and touched him, "Oh, he's cold as ice. Quick now, drag him in out of here and let's shut the door.

Instinctively, Sarah dropped the rifle and moved to help; first by shutting out the storm and then dragging her unwanted guest over toward the fire. The white man could say nothing, so exhausted was he, and they fed him luke warm water and tried to rub down his woolen clothes to get some circulation in. The commotion had awakened the boys, and Sam came over to stare wide-eyed at the living white man before him who looked like a ghost, he was so pale.

Though she was old, Reena still moved with strength, and was even stronger in her voice as she told Sarah what to do to get the man's circulation going.

"Mama Reena, he's a stranger and I bet he's a paddy-roller too! Out there hunting our folk," she said as she pointed out the door.

"Shush, now," Reena said to Sarah, "we all God's own. He's been blown to us for some purpose, I'm sure.

"Now when a man is frozen, when he gets his circulation back, he swells up, and this white man is swelling all over. A dark man goes gray when he is feelin' poorly, and a white man gets see-through blue," she said. "Is that his color, woman, or not?"

"The man is dying," thought Sarah, "why are we doing this for him."

Reena, however, was a woman possessed. She stripped him down and rubbed him with mustard so hard that she herself was sweating, even in the cold. Gradually, the man's breaths became more relaxed and he clearly was getting some life back to him. His boots were still on him and Reena demanded that Sarah help take them off. They had to cut the boots off of him, and when Reena touched the toes, she asked Sarah what color they was.

"Look black," Sarah said.

"Oh, devil is it," said Reena, "if they don't turn, we'll have to cut 'um."

As he slowly groaned, Sarah leaned over the man once more and said, "Sir, what is your name? Who are you?"

With the bit of strength that the man had left, he was able to utter one word "Hoggen".

Chapter XIX

Unwanted Guest

"Fitful dreams, that's what he have," cooed Reena to Sarah. "What fitful, frightful things he must be thinking about."

Sarah looked at the man lying on Reena's bed twitching in a deep slumber and she just nodded her head.

The storm lasted four days and then passed. Excepts for bits of water, the white man simply laid in bed with Reena tending to him day and night. Sarah tried as she could to unburden herself with this unwanted guest. Little William and Samuel were mesmerized by the white man and would stare at him constantly.

Sarah dug out from under the snow as best she could, to tend the animals, but far as it looked, they were covered in a deep blanket of snow all around.

Samuel got up one morning and stood over the man now lying with his head on a pillow.

"Mammy, Reena," he said, "Mammy, Reena, the man openin' his eyes!"

At that point, Reena reached out her arms, and said, "Well come here and bring me to him, boy."

Reena knelt down beside the man whose eyes were flickering, but he wasn't saying anything.

"Mister, Mister! You know you almost froze out there? But we brought you in and thawed you good. Can you speak?"

Hoggen moved his mouth, but nothing came out. His lips were cracked like dried, broken paint, like he was practicing to say something, but couldn't.

"You said something called 'Hoggen'. Is that your name?" Finally, he spoke clear as day, "Yes, it is, good woman. Please now help me to sit up, will ya. I'm thinkin' I'm going to have ta relieve myself."

At that, Samuel giggled.

"He talk funny, too, Mammy Reena."

"Yes, he do," said Reena, but she helped him up just the same.

"If ya please, I'm Jack Hoggen. And might I ask ya, where in God's earth am I," he rasped.

"Well, you're in Missouri, sir," said Reena. "At the Cooper farm. Why?" she asked, "Where do you want to be?"

"Dear, Lady, right now I'm glad to be anywhere," he said. "I can't move my legs, and I can't move my toes!" he said with alarm.

"You calm down, there Mr. Hoggen. Don't excite yourself so. You got the bite, is all, on your toes. If you can't feel them, don't move, don't move."

At that, she had Samuel run get the pan for Mr. Hoggen.

Just then, Sarah opened the door and a blast of cold air blew into the room.

"Oh," she said sourly, "our guest is up."

"Yes," said Reena, "he's doing mighty fine. His name is Hoggen and he was just telling us where he's from, now wasn't you Mr. Hoggen."

Hoggen startlingly said, "Ah, yes, I guess I was. I'm, well, I'm from Ireland, you see, and I come to E Merica to New Orleans. I'm a horseman by living and I was coming up the river to meet a horse trader. I was going to work breakin' horses and sell 'em on what they call the Santa Fe trail."

"But was you by yourself?" Sarah said. "How'd you end up out here?"

"Well, an altercation arose. A disagreement," said Hoggen, "between me and another gentleman. And seeing as how he was in much greater friendship with the riverboat captain, they disembarked me."

At that, Sarah shook her head. "You mean they threw you off the Riverboat?

"Exactly," he said quietly.

"Are you some kind of a card cheat?" she said, "Is that what you are?"

"Oh, no, no, no, dear lady," he said, "It's nothing quite as romantic as that. No, ye see, a man and I had a political disagreement, ye might say. But please," he said, "Seeing as how I can't properly stand right now, I would at least like to shake yur hand and thank ya for savin' me life."

At that, Hoggen reached out his long thin arms and took Sarah by her hand and squeezed it.

His hands were thin and cool, and Sarah thought they were almost the hands of a tall woman. Sarah introduced herself and Samuel and little Willy.

Reena spoke up, "Mr. Hoggen, you a lucky man even to be alive, but we still not so sure about your feet."

Sarah spoke quickly, "The snow's so deep, you best to wait a day before you go," she said.

At that, Reena jumped in, "He can't go now! Why, the bite's so bad, we might have to cut off them toes!"

"My toes!" yelled Hoggen. "Oh, no, no, no. You're not gonna cut off me toes, no. That just won't do," he said. At that, he tried to stand up, but fell back, as his feet didn't give him balance yet.

Sarah let out a sigh. "Well," she said, "we'll see about what Mama Reena can do to doctor you here, but you better listen to her. Now I gotta go back and get Judy some feed.

As she walked back out the door, Sarah was thinking to herself, "Another burden, good God, another burden."

Chapter XX

The Wait For Spring

"You sure look better," Florence said to Abraham as he sat up. "You've been drinking a lot of the Sassafras tea. That's good. It will help your spirit and brings back your energy.

Abraham was lying on a blanket on a dirt floor. It was a wooden cabin, and the fire was the only light in the room.

"Thans, mish," he said, "I'm peelin' mus better."

Outside, he could hear the wind howling and the sounds of a big storm. Florence saw Abraham looking around and decided to tell him.

"We are in a great storm, and my father says we will stay here through winter and not trade for a while. He says that if the storms come early like this, it will be a hard winter."

Abraham tried to speak as best he could, but it was so hard, all he could say was, "M' famile, peese, I'm beggin' you to hep."

At that, Florence touched her fingertips to his lips and pushed them together.

"Don't talk too much. Mother said you have to give your jaw a chance to heal, or it might never come back. Don't worry," she said, "I will take good care of you. Cherokee women are good at that. You are a nice color brown," she said matter of factly.

Abraham looked into her bright eyes and realized that, at

this point, speaking with her would do no good.

Just then, John Nave came to the door and Florence jumped back away from Abraham.

"Florence!" Nave said, "Go to our house now that you have brought this man his food."

Abraham looked at Nave and attempted to speak to him again, "Howth long hive been here?" he said.

"What?" Nave asked. "What is it you want to know?"

Abraham spread his arms wide and pointed to the ground and nodding his head.

"Oh, how long," said Nave. "We were on the trail many days, and four of those days you were in dream sleep. It's been another two months and a now you are coming out of your fever. My daughter tells me some of your tale. Tell me, what is your name?"

"Athrahan," Abraham said as best as he could.

"She tells me that, too. She is young, you know. Young girls like stories. She likes you." At that point, Nave looked down directly into Abraham's eyes. "Do you know what I mean?"

"Yesh, sur, I do. I tellin' you the truth. I free man."

"We Cherokee understand. We know the white man. Cherokees have been slave to the white man, too. If your tale is true or not, there is nothing we can do for you now. You'll just have to wait and get better. For now, Florence has claimed you for the loss of her brother to the whites. You have to work here, like everyone else. Come spring, and your word is true, we will talk about the price to bring you back to your people."

"In the thring?" he said, "I can't waith 'til . . ."

John reached and touched Abraham's shoulder, and said something in a language that Abraham did not understand. Then in English, Nave said, "We will all die if we try to cross this country in the dead of winter. Do you understand?"

Abraham slumped his shoulders. "Yesh."

"Good. Now eat your food that my daughter has brought and rest."

"Spring," Abraham thought to himself. "What will my Sarah do!"

Chapter XXI

The Green Isle

The sound of children's laughter could be heard even though the door was closed on her cabin. Sarah was trying to bring wood into the house and could hear the screeching laughter of her two little boys.

Inside, the now stronger Hoggen, was hobbling about on a stick, using it like a crutch and trying to get the boys to jump by tickling them.

"Samuel," he said, "Have I told ya about the tickle fairy! Come over here and let me show ya what he looks like. Now, he's a little bit here in the palm of me hand, right here, now. Come on over here."

Without even touching him, little Samuel would screech with laughter, and run about.

Sarah had shaved Hoggen's face, although he had asked that he keep his moustache and the hair below his chin, so he looked like, as he told Sarah, "a Spanish conquistador." Sarah didn't know what he was talking about, but didn't ask. Never had Sarah seen the likes of Hoggen. He could talk more than anyone she'd ever met. All day long, Hoggen would tell tales and stories and Reena seemed bewitched by him.

One morning, Reena said to Sarah, "You know, Mr. Hoggen, he's from that Ireland and he said they call that place the green isle and . . ."

Sarah had had enough. "Mama Reena, between you and that

strange talking white man, I can't get any peace in this house!" Reena said, "Well, you know, he's just . . ."

"I know," Sarah said, "And he's your guest now, but he's a stranger, too."

Reena replied, "Girl, just ask the man. He'll tell you 'bout hisself. He got a good heart."

"I just don't trust white men," she said in a somber tone, "except Rene."

Hoggen had hobbled over to help clean up after dinner and for a reason even she didn't know, she decided to sit down and find out about Mr. Hoggen and why he was really in Missouri.

"How did you get here, and why are you here, if you don't mind me askin'?" Sarah blurted out bluntly.

"Well, seeing how you saved me life, I suppose I can confide in ya that I didn't come to America really of my own free will."

"Seems few do," said Sarah as she smiled a bit.

"I am from western Ireland. It's a beautiful green land, but hard livin' and harder still because of the English. They own everything and make us sharecrop our own land. Those of us that want to see a change are called Finneans. We want our people to rule their own land."

"So how'd you get here, then, if you're some kind of fine man," Sarah said.

"No, 'Finneans'," he corrected. "I escaped the wrath of the law," he said, sailing from Bantry Bay, I come to New Orleans as a lot of Irish come. "It's Irish that build canals and the levies for wages and bread. But me, I came to escape. No, I'm not a digger. For me, horses is what I do best and I had heard of a job for a man by the name of McCormick and I come meet him and to break horses up here. But after I got thrown off that steamboat and started walking and that snow storm hit, I got lost and found my way to your door step."

Sarah leaned over, "So why are you runnin' from the law? What'd you do?"

At that point, Hoggen leaned closer to her and his big blue eyes got narrow, "I did something a man should never do. God help me, I killed someone," he said. "I took another's life." Sarah shuddered. "You what?"

"It's a long story."

"Well, I'm not a woman to keep a killer in my home, so you better tell me," she said.

Chapter XXII

The Horse Race

"My mother's name was Molly Hoggen. My sister is Katherine Hoggen. My father was drowned when I was 15, fishing off the Aran Islands which is off the coast of Ireland.

"Ever since I was a boy, I loved the horses. I saw them galloping in the fields and many times I dreamed I was one, too. Just like them, I wanted to be proud, strong, fast and noble. When I was 13, I got a job as a stable boy. I was working shoveling horse manure and rubbing down the long legged horses of Mr. Edward Thornton. My best friend, Sweeney, worked for him, too! He owned the largest farm in County Clare. Thornton's son, Stanton, was a year older than me. Thornton was a cold hearted man, but his son, Stanton's heart, was even colder.

"Stanton treated me like dirt and though I tried my best not to get in his way, he fancied himself a horseman and I had to help him train his stallion, Aegis. I had been working for Thornton there a good long time. Helped bring many a race horse to the winning circle, and finally, I had been able to bring my mother Molly, and my sister, Katherine, to rent a small shack on the Thornton farm.

"By now, my sister had grown to be a beautiful young woman of 17. She had reddish blonde hair, all long and full. Her skin was white like ivory and her eyes were blue as the spring sky."

Hoggen sighed, "May I have a bit of water?"

At that point Reena came over. "Go on, go on, tell your story. Let me get you some water," she said.

"Oh, yes," Hoggen said. "Yes, well then, where was I? Oh, yes."

"There was a big race to run and the Thornton boy, who was now a man, was riding. It was going to be in Dublin and he brought me with him. Though my sister was an innocent girl, she too, longing to see a big city like Dublin, desired to go too. And so, at Stanton's request, we all three went there together."

"I can remember his sweet talk as if it were before me now."

"'Katherine', he said, 'you'll love the big city. Come now, sit up in the first train carriage with me.'

"Except this Stanton had more on his mind than racing the horse. So off we went to the big race. A week later, when we were at the stables outside the track where his new gray gelding, Padric, was going to race, my sister came up to me and told me of what had happened to her. Stanton had taken . . ., well . . . he had taken advantage of her, and so I went to see him."

"Aye, we did," said Stanton, "but it's not what you think. Your sister, she came for me, not the other way around. The tart wants to marry well."

"Don't call my sister a tart!" I said, "Don't you ever."

"Listen. Don't be stupid. It was nothing," Stanton spit out.

"Katherine tried to tell me to leave it be, but later that night I went to the pub. May God help me, I did. And Stanton boasting about his horse racing and then about my sister.

"I took her and booted her well! She screamed for it, the cheap Irish whore," he laughed.

"I couldn't help but call him outside.

"You think you can take me?" Stanton said.

"Then he threw the first punch at me. I struck him with a blow and in his drunken stupor, he fell and cracked his head on a cobblestone, blood poring from his head. Later that night, he died."

"Oh." said Sarah, "It sounds like you didn't try to kill him. It was just a fight between two men."

Reena chimed in, "Lord, yes, and he had it coming to him, too! Them's that got the station above always takin' liberties with women."

"What happened?" Sarah said, "After that?"

"An Irishman killing an Englishman, I couldn't get a fair trial. And so, I hid out as best I could and my mother and some of my friends were able to get me to Bantry Bay to sail to America. Last I saw of my home was my mother waving good-bye to me. I'll never see her again," Hoggen said, looking out the cabin window in a daze, "Nor my Green Isle."

"You poor man," sighed Reena.

"Hmmm, yes. Bad things happen," said Sarah, "To all of us."

Chapter XXIII

Claidhim

Much to his happiness, and that of his feet as well, Hoggen's toes got better. Though he was still hob-blin' on his "long stick," as he called it, he was soon out and about walking with the boys.

"Miss Reena won't be chopping you off!" he said pointing to his feet on the first morning he could stand on his own two legs.

"Samuel, will ya help me find me sack which I lost in that storm? I'll give ya a penny," Hoggen said to the little boy.

"What's in it, Mister Hoggen?" the little boy said excitedly.

"Oh, it's my special sword, my Claidhim."

"What that?" he said.

"Well," said Hoggen, "Long before the English, who I told you about, ruled our land, we were a free people. The Claidhim was sort of a man's special sword for fightin', for workin', and for doing a hundred different things. It was what a Finnean carried with himself, ya see. Now, if you help me find mine, I'll tell ya how I discovered this old sword in the ruins of an old castle." In the slush of the melting snows, it didn't take little Samuel long to find the leather sack a half mile or so from the cabin.

"There she is," said Hoggen. "Here's your penny now."
He unfurled the leather and there was a sword with a silver cross bar and ring in it's handle. When he picked it up, Hoggen

96

smiled.

"Aye, my Claidhim," he said, "I thought for a while we were both lost."

"Well," said Samuel, "how'd you find it?"

"Oh, yes, yes, the story of how I found it. Well, my sister and I were great gatherers of wild flowers. One day, in the ruins of an old castle, we were hunting for wild flowers to bring home to my mother when something caught my eye beneath two great stones. I thought it was a rabbit hutch and maybe I'd find some babies, so I started digging it out. But what it really was, was an ancient tomb. Well, in that tomb was a broken hilt of a sword. Not my Claidhim, but another. And so my sister and I kept digging and we found more pieces of these broken warring tools. Then I came upon her, my Claidhim, and brought her home. I told nobody about it for a long time. I thought our landlord might take it as an antiquity."

"What's that mean?" said Samuel.

"Oh, I thought the owner of the land may take it from me because it was old and had value."

"Oh. Well, did he take it?"

"No, lad, I never revealed her. But now we better get back to your little cabin and we will tell some more stories there. I'll race you for a penny!" said Hoggen, and Samuel shot off like a bullet out of a rifle.

"Hoggen wrapped up his sword and stuck it in his trouser belt and hobbled back to the cabin.

"It was good luck that I found it," he said to himself. "Maybe good luck will be on me for this time."

Chapter XXIV

He Who Sees The Spirit

Several weeks later, Rene came to look in on Sarah. He rode with a friend, an Osage Indian whose name was too long to pronounce, so Rene just called him Doc.

"Doc be a special man," Rene once told Abraham, "and he has 'strong medicine,' for that is what he brought to his people. Before I knew him, one night in a dream he saw a great crow who told him to leave his people and come to the white's and there he'd find a way to save his people. While he was away, the tribe was hit with the fever and many perished. When Doc got back, he nursed the survivors. Saved them. Then the crow came again in his dream and told him to leave again. We met many years ago and he and I became friends. He told me his story, and I started calling him 'Doc'," said Rene, "He can fix any man's ails with his herbs, potions and fits of praying."

At first Rene and Doc were very cold to Hoggen, but Reena made Doc lighten by telling him about Hoggen running away from Ireland and the awful things that had befallen him. The Indian whispered something into Rene's ear and Rene looked strangely back at him.

Riding back, Rene asked, "Doc, why did you whisper that in my ear?"

Doc turned to him and said, "I could feel it. That white man's spirit is not right here. He is of two worlds. He is heading for trouble, for he does not belong here. He must return to his true spirit."

At that, the great French man nodded his head, for he knew from his years of being with Doc that what he saw often came true.

"What is he to do, Doc?" asked Renee.

"That white man is splitting like a tree. He leans to both sides of his path. Both human and something else."

"What?" said Renee.

"What, I cannot tell now," said Doc. "Give me time and I will, but not now.

"You see too much in men, Doc.

"I see nothing that is not told to me by the sacred spirit."

"Yes, Doc, I know. But your world scares me anyway."

"Your world scares me, also. What is living for me does not live for the whites. My people are going blind to the old ways. The whites will make us blind to all that. It will make you blind, too! Beware, my friend, not all change is for the good. Even more for my people."

"I'm sorry, Doc," Rene said in a quiet tone.

"Me, too, Rene. Me too."

Chapter XXV

Finneans and Goats

"Tell me some more, Hoggen, will ya?"

"What about, Samuel?"

"Tell me about them swords and them Freenians, too."

"No, no, boy. They're Finneans. They were the folks, you know, the warriors of the old time of Ireland. Before the Irish were conquered by the Normans, and before the English twisted politics and treaties and we lost our land and our freedom, when Irish Kings ruled the lands, the Finneans was the noble fighters for the rights of the people. They protected the lands from the invaders. I believe my Claidhim might have belonged to one of them, you know.

"Was you one?" Samuel asked, with his eyes all wide.

"Oh, not like that, no. I did join a group, though. And we called ourselves Finneans to honor those Irish from long ago. But we was tryin' to free the new Ireland. Make it one country again. That's why we called ourselves the Finneans."

"Was you a fightin' them? Is that why you come to America?"

"Oh, no, I wasn't fightin' for Ireland, I was fightin' over my sister. Truth be told, Samuel, I never did much fightin'. Maybe I should have done more, but it wasn't in me."

"What'd you do, then?" he asked.

"Oh, we'd do things mostly to annoy the English. Let the people know that there was some that didn't just bend over to the rule. But then I was asked to do something that I wouldn't do, and I kinda fell out of favor with them for a while."

"What happened? What did you do wrong?"

"Lad, it wasn't what I did, it was what I wouldn't do. You see, we were in Belfast for stake races. The Thorntons had a beautiful mare to run and I'd been banking on the win. But anyway, I gets the information on a high sign from the group. There was a parade in Belfast held in July, you know, the Orangemen they called themselves, loyal to the crown. Anyway, I was tending the horses, when I get the high sign. Teddy Mahoney comes and says they're going to make a ruckus of the whole parade. Make a statement, he says, to show that the Irish are still alive in the north. 'Well, what's the rub, then?' I asked him.

"'Tis their goat," he said, "The one they parade at the start of every parade. That stubborn nanny goat of theirs. We're going to tar it and burn it before the parade. That will throw them off."

I said, "But I don't want to burn no goat! What's the goat ever done to deserve that kind of burning?"

"Ah, Jesus," says Teddy Mahoney, "You eat lamb, don't ya? What did the lamb ever do to ya? This is a political statement, ya fool!"

"Well when the time come, I just couldn't do it. Goat burning just wasn't in me, Sam. It was against my nature to hurt an animal like that, even if it was for political reasons."

"So what'd they do?" Samuel said, nodding his head in agreement.

"I was kinda punished, so to speak."

"But I thought they helped you escape," Samuel said.

101

"They did, lad. After I killed that Englishman, I was a hero for them. Fleeing from the law and all. I was kinda famous. Imagine, famous for that, huh?" and at that, Hoggen shook his head and looked down.

"People see what they want and use what they can for their own purpose, you know. But me, I just didn't quite fit into that. I don't make my road, I just kinda go down it, taking it where it leads me."

Samuel grabbed Hoggen's hand, "I'm glad it led you here."

"Aye, me too, lad, me too."

"Hoggen?"

"Yeah?"

"What happened to that goat?"

"They burned it. Without me."

"Poor goat."

"Yes, lad, poor goat. And the parade went on anyway."

Chapter XXVI

The Tinker's Daughter

Mama Reena was sitting on her chair on the front porch. Abraham had actually made her the chair and given it to her for her birthday. Most days when Sarah was in fixing supper, Reena would sit and rock with her eyes closed and her head thrown back. She did this in the late afternoon when it was still a bit warm, but not so hot as it was earlier in the afternoon. Reena said this was the best time to sit, before the biters and the flies would come out and cause everyone to go inside.

Hoggen came up towards the house, and seeing her rocking back and forth with her eyes closed, humming some tune to herself, he stood there for a moment watching. Mama Reena sensed somebody was there and she kind of stopped her humming and cocked her head sideways like a dog would do when he hears a sound in the distance.

Hoggen cleared his throat, "Miss Reena, my mother loved to rock in her chair, just like you're doin', in front of our turf fire at night.

Mama Reena relaxed when she heard this. "Did she? What kind of woman was your mama, Mister Hoggen?"

"She was lovely, humorous, and smart. She loved to make me jams in the summertime. She said the best thing about summer was making the jams to spread on the bread in the winter. My Dah . . . my father, used to say her eyes were dark pools of blue cream."

"Is that so," Mama Reena said. "It's good that you've got nice memories of your mama."

Out of nowhere Hoggen said, "Do you know the walking people, Miss Reena?"

"Can't say as I do," she said.

"They're Tinkers. That's what they were called in their day. My mother was a Tinker's daughter. My father met her out at a fair in Ballyliffin. He was a fisherman from the coast selling the salmon and she the knifes her Tinker father had made. The Tinkers. The travelers as they're called sometimes, too. They traverse all over Ireland, fixing things and selling their wears. Never staying in one place."

"You do say," Mama Reena said. "Well I had not much education myself, 'cepting the good book and what you learn on the plantation, but travelers . . ."

". . . are like seeds out there," Hoggen suddenly started again, "you see in the fields, blowin' wherever the wind pushes them."

"What's your mama's name, again?" Mama Reena asked.

"Molly was her name," Hoggen said this and looked far away over the top of the roof of the house as he said it.

"You know her family barely spoke to her after my father married her. Because he wasn't a Tinker."

"Ain't families funny," Mama Reena said. "You know, the Lord just has you fall in love with whoever and sometimes it don't matter who they be. But that's his way."

Hoggen just kept to talking, "You know, Miss Reena, they built a cottage. Really just a thatched roof with straw rope. But there she'd rock, waitin' for her man, Jimmy, to come back from the sea. It was her best time, though. Before we were born, me and my sister, they'd go to the fairs together and he'd be sellin' his salted salmon, and even fishing up at the river Moy in Donegal. She said it reminded her of her childhood, bundled together by the fire, living by the side of the road with her Jimmy, all free on the road.

"Mister Hoggen, you're spinning my head with all the names and the places you're talking about, but I sure likes your story. Tell me more."

"Do you really want to know?"

"Course I do," she said.

"Well, first me, then three years later Katherine came along. My father worked as hard as he could fishing. Sometimes he'd work the big lands of the lords' plantations, just like you got here. The great lords, taking the Irish's land. The English took and gave them, as my Dah used to say, 'Sure jack, me boy, go become a priest before you work for a guinea a month on some Scot's land.' Funny, you know, Miss Reena, but I loved to visit him in those summers working on the big lands, the richest lands were so beautiful. And the horses. Oh, but heavens the horses were beautiful. All running free in the fields, so cared for and tended whilst us poor Irish sat squat, eating potatoes and watching the best oats go to the horses."

Mama Reena started nodding her head, "Seems like you and me, Mister Hoggen, both seen a lot of plantations." At that she cackled. "'Course I ain't seen much in more 'n ten years, but I still see enough," she said. "But you had them big places with no nigras?"

"No, Miss Reena, just the Irish. Two hundred years we've been run over, the best lands to those that took the 'black oath' to the King. Poor lowlander Scotts and English loyal to the crown. But we knew we'd revolt some day, and some day we will. But until then, they give the land to the strangers and they guard us and keep us in place and if you step out of line, oh, how they step on ya. They step on ya hard. Real hard.

"Miss Reena, I guess in some ways I'm just a failure, for even I couldn't be the revolutionary that I had hoped I could, to change things. The things I hoped I could."

"Really," Mama Reena said, "you don't seem like that kind of man."

"I remember the meetings myself. 'Join the Finneans!' they'd say. 'Free Ireland.' But when you joined, they used you. When it was done, you're left looking over your shoulder your whole life, waiting for the law," Hoggen said.

"The sport of horses more than the politics was what I cared about. I am ashamed to say, Miss Reena, I was so glad when we took to the road for races with Thornton's son. It gave me an excuse not to do the 'little jobs' I was asked to do."

He shook himself at the thought. "Happier am I to work an Englishman's race horse than free on my own land! What a failure!"

"Ain't nobody a failure who follows their passion."

"And still, Miss Reena," Hoggen went on, "with my father gone and drowned and my mother still there, I don't know what's happened to her. To this day, I bet she's rockin' herself every night now, cryin' as she's never seein' me nor her husband again." At that, Hoggen's voice started to crack.

Miss Reena said, "I'm sure she's fine. We all have kin that we'll never see again. Lord's sure, that's a slave's curse, you know. Sold and gone. But keep her in your mind's eye, Mister Hoggen. You know what we say?"

"What's that, Miss Reena?"

"You decide who's your family. Ain't no man can take that

away. We do, too. Slaves make our own family no matter what the white man tries to kill. Cousins and friends is all family. See what I mean?"

"Aye, Miss Reena, I feel the same way. We are not that different at all."

"Mister Hoggen, you becoming a part of this family. How's that now?"

"I'm honored, Miss Reena."

Sarah stood at the door listening to the conversation, even though Hoggen and Mama Reena never saw her. She was about to say something, but stood there silently.

"He is a good man," she thought, "A good man for sure."

Chapter XXVII

The Agreement

For the first months, Sarah was still a bit stand-offish and formal towards Hoggen, but as he got better and she came to know this humorous Irish man, she thought he was a good distraction for her boys.

Spring was upon her and though she was every day looking for Abraham to come home, the time had come for her to say good-bye to her man. Her man been gone for eight months now. So, one morning she picked up Abraham's fiddle, took the boys and Reena and walked to the river and there said her final good-byes to her man.

"Dear Lord, hold my Abraham in your arms. May he rest wherever he is in peace and bless his soul."

"Amen," said Reena.

"Amen," said little Samuel.

Hoggen, with his head bowed, said a silent amen as well.

The tears running down her face, she walked back to the cabin and Hoggen quietly walked beside her. "Do you know, Miss Sarah, I've been helping as best I can these months. My toes is better and so I can start doing more hard work for you. It's the least I can do for you saving my life."

"Mister Hoggen, I thank you for your offer, but you ain't a farmer."

"I know, but I can do anything else. I can carry, I can ride."

"You read?" said Sarah.

"I can read well. 'Tis one of my great passions."

"Then here's what I want you to do," Sarah said. "You teach my Samuel how to read, give him the tools to be what the white man don't want him to be and help where you can and let me do my farming. That's an agreement that I can live with.

"Oh, and one more thing. Now that you're healthy enough to walk around as you appear to be, you'll sleep in the barn." At that, Sarah pointed toward the wooden barn.

Hoggen laughed. "The barn it is!" he said. "Things will get better for ya, Sarah. I know they will."

Sarah handed Hoggen a bible that Reena kept, although Reena couldn't see nor read it. "Take this, too," she said, handing Abraham's fiddle to Hoggen, hold this while I blow my nose and walk alone for a while."

Sarah had no idea now what the new spring year would bring, but she knew at least that her boy would get some education to make a better life for himself someday.

After moving to the barn, Hoggen set a warm place to sleep near Sarah's horse, Judy, and as she watched him, Sarah could see what Hoggen meant by his special ways with the horses. He cooed to Judy as he brushed and fed her. You could see the delight in her horse eyes as they left the corral.

"The first lesson starts after supper," she called to Hoggen.

Sarah asked "Do you think you could ride the horse down to the trading post."

"I could, if I knew how to get there," he said.

"It's easy enough," she said. "Go south of our land and there you'll see sycamores along the creek. Follow them to the river and then south to the ferry. Across the river, you will find Rene's trading post."

"Consider it done."

The next morning he was on Judy heading off to the trading post.

"I'll be back, now, don't you worry," he said to Sarah.

"Mr. Hoggen, I've stopped worrying along time ago 'bout men telling me they'll be back, but bring back my horse, you hear!"

At that, Hoggen laughed as he galloped Judy down to the green sycamore saplings growing along the creek, and off to the trading post.

Chapter XXVIII

The Ghost Horse

Hoggen heard the story of the wild horse from Rene. She would come at night and take away the stock horses.

No one saw her except as a shadow in the evening melting into the blackness of the night. Once Rene saw only the white diamond mark on her forehead as she raced with two brood mares.

As the herd grew, some swear that they'd seen them in the distance, an enormous size . . . living in this wild land. It was this way out here, the weak died, the strong survived and put their blood into the colts who grew and challenged to lead the herd.

Hoggen was daydreaming these thoughts as he rode across the valley floor, on Judy. This land was wilder than Ireland, but terribly beautiful.

As the sun was drifting toward the horizon, Hoggen saw in the distance two plumes of dust. They were parallel, heading away from him. They sky was turning the pinkish-red it does in the evenings, and he could tell that the two horses were riderless. It must be part of the wild herd, he thought to himself. He hoped against hope that perhaps it would be the mare.

Heading to the trading post for the supplies that Sarah had asked him to get was forgotten as he dug a spur into Judy, and cut diagonally across the bluffs to catch the plumes in the distant horizon.

"This is America," Hoggen said to himself, "watching a wild horse run across an unfenced area. There in the wild land, an animal free of humans, living the life of his ancestors."

Hoggen made good time as he came over a bluff after galloping Judy hard. He saw below him two horses in a ravine. They had slowed and were nuzzling each other and pawing the earth.

"Easy, Judy," said Hoggen, "give her easy, now." Hoggen slowed the horse and stayed down wind. The sun was setting further, and the horizon was a grayish light now. He eased his horse away, and watched as the black mare and the chestnut brown stallion stopped, bending down and grazing, flipping their long tails back and forth against the evening insects buzzing about them. He could see why the farmers called her the Ghost Horse. As the gray of night was creeping in, he could see how invisible her coat would be at night, as she thievingly snuck around to steal more stock for her herd.

This was their rendezvous point, Hoggen thought. The stallion waiting patiently, she off to more farms to snatch their stock. He, dutifully the husband, patiently waiting for her return. Never in his life had Hoggen come across such larceny.

Of course, stallions would come and poach a man's farm stock, but the mare doing the stealing was unnatural.

As night fell, she gave her stallion a nod and took off. She moved quickly, and Hoggen followed as best he could. At first, following her at some distance, but later, as by necessity, moving closer as night fell, and viewing her only in the silvery moonlight.

"Good God, what a magnificent creature she is," Hoggen said to Judy.

She was fifteen hands high and a thousand pounds, at least. Every muscle and fiber moving in unison as she walked and then galloped across the prairie floors. It was clear to Hoggen that she was not a pure Spanish pony, like many of the well-stocked mustangs of these plains. The way she held her head high and the look of her tail told him she was Arabian in her bloodline. The way she moved her legs and paced herself, he knew she was fashioned in part by man and in part by God.

This was why she was so familiar with the ways of man, she was not borne wild, she was a convert. Hoggen knew the passion a convert brings to a cause. "Come with me, come with me," she'd say to the corralled stock of some farmer, "come and be free." He was startled when he realized he was talking out loud and hoped that his voice wouldn't carry so far ahead. "Yes," he said to himself, "that's what she tells the fenced in, the corralled, the mares and geldings." The Ghost Horse, she came at night, unafraid of man, knowing of his fences and corrals, and determined to bring more stock for her grateful stallion and the herd which she was creating with him.

He was startled from his thoughts when she veered south from her western course. Hoggen knew that she was heading for the Owens' farm. Sarah had told Hoggen about the Owens. "Good folk," she told him. He stopped following the mare at that point, trying to recollect what Rene had told him about a series of creek beds that ran north to south in this area, and tried to cut through so as to meet her at Owens' spread. He rode little Judy hard as hard as he could, and luckily, he got there before the Ghost. He waited in the dark at Owens' place for the sound of some movement by the corral, but not wanting to startle the Owens' family, nor alarm them, he kept to himself and said nothing.

Gabe Owens only had a brood mare with a young foal, and a mule. He couldn't afford to lose any of his stock. Hoggen took it upon himself to be the guardian for the evening. When the moon had reached its height and was beginning to set again, he could hear stirring over by the corral, and then he saw her. The black mare slowly sashayed up to the corral, making short little bowing head movements, and quietly snorting to draw attention to the mare. Some kind of exchange happened, a horse talk which only horses must know, and then he watched the ghost black mare start nudging the rope latch over the corral post, taking it up to the top of the post. She then threw her weight against the gate, jumping back and watched as it bounced against the post and slowly opening up.

There it was, he thought to himself. "Thief."

She had opened up the corral, and suddenly the black and tan mare and the colt were out. The two trotted into the evening and the Ghost was turning with her new catch. The rope Hoggen had thrown around her with such skill was so quick that she had barely time to rear up on her hind quarters and scream in defiance.

At that point, Hoggen shouted out, "Gabe, Gabe, come out, the mare is stealing your Sheila and colt. Come quick, come quick! Gabe!" Awakened to the evening roust, Gabe Owens came out in his long-johns, with a rifle in his hand and his two boys loping behind him.

Meanwhile, Hoggen was holding on for dear life as the mare rocked and bucked and kicked and jumped trying to uncoil the rope from her neck. The commotion frightened the colt and caused the mare to fight and stir and try and shield her young one. In short time, the boys were able to corral the two stock back. They took to aiding Hoggen to calm down the black fury as she tried to escape. Two more ropes came upon her, and she struggled still. For over a half an hour the sweat poured off her as Gabe, the boys and Hoggen held. She finally stopped and gave in to exhaustion, the rope and the strength of the men. Hoggen was able to yank her slowly into the corral and tie her strong. High strung, and clearly in distress, she jumped and kicked, but could not overcome the hard wood of the corral.

"Well, Mister Hoggen," said Gabe, "so you saved my horses, and for that I owe you a great favor. I'll go and shoot that she-devil right now!"

"No, no, man, look at her, look at her, she's magnificent, Gabe! You can't shoot her, I won't let ya." "Where I come from," Hoggen spoke low voiced to Gabe, "a horse like this should be running in Kilkinney or in the Galloway Stakes. No, man, let me keep her here 'til the morning. I'll stay by and make sure she doesn't break anything and tomorrow I'll take her to Sarah's."

Gabe's eyes bugged out of his face, "Hoggen, you're mad. She's been broken and returned wild. She'll be even more difficult to control. That's they way it is with these horses. She'll never let you be her master. They're fickle that way, I know. Shoot her now!"

"I won't," Hoggen said and the sternness in his voice made Gabe stop any further suggestion to the contrary.

Hoggen slept fitfully, for the mare stirred constantly, calling out, knowing that her stallion was out there. Calling out and hoping he'd come free her. Then she collapsed in a sullenness when, hour after hour, her mate did not come.

When daylight came the next morning, Hoggen's belief of her heritage was confirmed. It was her nose and ears, all Arab. A horse like this was bred for riding, for endurance and speed over the dunes of her ancient homeland. How in God's name a horse like this ended up in Missouri was a mystery. Somewhere someone was missing a beautiful horse.

The white diamond on her forehead stood out like a jewel on the neck of a princess. You are a Ghost so that is what I'll call you then: The Ghost Horse," Hoggen said to her.

"Easy, now, easy," he said in a soothing tone. "Ghost, be quiet now. Come, I won't let 'em hurt ya."

Her nostrils flared and she stomped her feet at first, but as he continued to talk, she didn't stir so, but stared at him. Her deep, dark eyes were watery and intelligent. She was looking at the little man, from her perspective, who had forced her back into man's world. She would find a way to escape, and he knew it, but he was determined to try and see exactly what kind of horse this The Ghost was.

Chapter XXIX

Indian Way

Water swirled. Two bodies thrashed against each other. Abraham felt himself drowning, his lungs burning for air. The white man's hands squeezed his throat, squeezing harder and harder and harder until there was nothing but blackness.

"No, no," he cried out loud, "No!"

Drew came running into the room where Abraham lay sleeping.

"Abraham! What's ya doing? You yelled out, now. What's going on?"

Abraham had a sweat on him and he sat up shaking his head like he was trying to get cobwebs off his hair.

"It's this dream I had. Me and that white man struggling in the water. I keep dreaming 'bout it over and over, like it won't go away. My head is pounding!"

Abraham's headaches still came almost every night, making him so dizzy he couldn't stand.

Drew shook his head, too, but in a knowing way. "You and that white man still in a fight. You and his spirit gotta come to some understanding. If I was you, I'd ask Tucker Grayson to help you. He's the spirit man here. You needs to find some kinda balance," said Drew getting up to fetch some water for Abraham.

Drew sat down again on his haunches with a cup of water in

117

his hand.

"Yes, siree. You see, I'm a killer. I've killed before. But you, you're not a killer. You have to let go of this, otherwise it will keep eatin' on ya."

"You're not a killer," said Abraham, "You're a hunter."

"Killin's killin," said Drew. "I've learned from the Cherokee that any time there's killin' done, things have to be set right, and you haven't set right with this man. Go see Grayson. They say he's learned his magic from the owls."

"The what?" said Abraham.

"The owls," said Drew. "That's the most powerful Indian help. They say the owls are the only ones that didn't sleep when God created the earth in seven days."

"This foolishness sure reminds me of something I heard once before," said Abraham, who thought of Scrimshaw and his bones. And then Abraham remembered how Scrimshaw foretold of his farm.

"I guess I better go see him."

Tucker Grayson still dressed in the old way with his turban and his colored shirt of vermillion. Abraham told him of the dreams, and the old medicine man stopped him in mid-sentence.

"You need to cleanse yourself in a sacred fire. I need you to get me white oak, sassafrass and red mulberry leaves."

Abraham watched as the old man bathed himself in the creek and read out loud from a small book he kept. These were the ancient words he said as he thanked the Great Sequoia who gave the Cherokee the alphabet to write down the ancient one's cures.

After building a fire, he cut Abraham's arm and had the blood drip into the ground near the fire.

"Drink the tea," Grayson said, then he was told by the old

man to thank the white man for dying so that Abraham could live and promise that balance would be restored one day by the clan of Abraham.

"What must I do now?" Abraham asked.

"It is done," said Grayson, "We Cherokee believe in balance above all things. A white man died. To balance, you must promise to give a life too. That is what you have done. You will have no more bad dreams.

"For the Cherokee, all is balance. Do not eat more than you need or kill more than you need to eat. A white man killed Florence's brother, and she takes you to balance the loss. That is the Cherokee way."

"But, I'm a free man," Abraham said. "Will I ever get free again?"

"You are of the whites, and not Cherokee. You must go before our tribal council to state your case, and if they agree, then Florence will have no claim for you."

That evening, before he went to sleep, Abraham thought about what Grayson had told him. He went to sleep that night and had no dreams of the white man trying to kill him.

The next day, he was up early and working when Drew came to him, clearly alarmed.

"Army calvary is comin'," Drew said. "Stay low and out of the way. Something's going on, I don't know what."

"What do you think it is?" Abraham asked.

"It's not good. The Indian Commissioner is here, too."

And so Abraham, not knowing what exactly to do, went back into the cabin, but kept the door open to over hear the conversation between the Captain and John Nave and the other elders.

"It's the law and we have to enforce it," said the

Calvaryman. "You've been here way over the two years you were given. Longer than needed for you to relocate."

"But this is our land by agreement," said Nave to the Commissioner, Harry Sturding. "Not now. The State of Missouri passed a law that said no Indians on these lands. Our new treaty will provide you safe passage to Arkansas and land there. You've got three days. Then we're coming and burning and clearing you out," clipped the calvaryman to Nave. They rode off and a cloud of dust and despair descended upon the village.

"What are they talking about?" Abraham asked Drew.

"Seems like the State of Missouri didn't want Indians and now we have to leave. Some kind of law passed in 1825. Even though we're the old people here," Drew said, "We have to leave to join other Cherokee in Arkansas."

"But, what about trading and getting me back to my family," Abraham asked.

"If I was you, I'd hurry up and talk to the council before we leave this land."

That night, over fried corn bread and jerked beaver, Abraham talked to Florence about how he could approach the council.

"First," said Florence, "the council must pick men who can decide what your fate will be. Second, someone must speak for you," she said, "I cannot speak for you because . . ."

"You won't speak for me because you want me to stay here. Grayson has told me about the Indian way."

"It is not just that," she said, "I want you to stay here because . . ."

She stopped mid-sentence and looked him in the eyes deeply.

"I just want you to stay," she said.

"Who, then, can speak for me? Will your father?"

"You can ask him, but he lost a son, as I told you."

"Can Drew speak for me?" Abraham asked.

"Although he is like you, he can. Who do you want to choose?"

"I'll choose Drew," Abraham said.

"Good, then. Tomorrow go with him to the council. But if they so decide that you are to be here, then you cannot leave, or they will hunt you down."

"I understand," Abraham said, "I understand." And though he tried not to think about it, he said little prayers to himself.

Chapter XXX

The Warrior Trial

The Cherokee required that someone speak for Abraham and Drew did his best to explain to the four warriors who were to rule on Abraham's fate with the tribe.

"This man was found in chains, but he was already free and was known by the white man. He can't be taken to balance between the Cherokee and the white for the loss of Comes-With-A-Feather and their family. I've told the story before of where he came from. It rings true to me, and if you think true to yourselves, it would make sense to you.

"I came here a runaway slave, and would never go back. I am now more Cherokee than Negro. But this one wants to go back, even though he does not have the papers which I told you would show you he is a free man. He risks everything to go back for his family. Is this not a sign that he speaks truthfully and is not the property of another?"

John Nave then stood up.

"I know not of whether this story is true," said Nave. "I do know that every time a white man speaks, there are two truths. One is his truth and one is the real truth. This black man tells me a story, but I find him in chains when he says he is free.

"My son is buried now only a year, and still the family waits for peace to come. Comes-With-A-Feather found him and says that this will give us the peace. As between a stranger and my daughter, I believe my daughter."

At that, Grayson turned to Nave.

"Then bring her here and let us see what she says."

At that, Florence came in to speak with the group.

"What do you say of this?" Grayson asked. "These warriors must decide for our people — either to believe that this man is free and to let him go again or to let you take him for your family because of what the white man has done."

"I found him in the river," Florence said. "He's a runaway slave, and like many, he was in chains. You know some Cherokee own slaves like the white man. I do not want a slave like the white man, but our family needs to find peace for the loss and I believe that this man is a runaway slave who will stay with us and be like a brother to me. Yet he does not act like a runaway. For all he tells me is that he wants is to return home.

"Some say in the old days we would kill to make it right. But now we do not. And that is why I took him and let him live. But I cannot make him stay if his heart is truly somewhere else, and I cannot think why he would lie so."

"Well, I can," said John Nave. "He lies so he can escape us, too, and find his own freedom. That is why he lies."

Drew stood up at this point. "We are a people who now must move again because of the white. We are on our way to the Arkansas territory now and leaving behind all that we have become accustomed to here, as you old people say. Let this one Negro help us to move. Earn his right to leave by paying us back for the loss of the boy. If he does, then I say let him go or stay as he pleases.

"Leave us all," said Grayson. "We will make our decision shortly.

At that, the warriors talked amongst themselves and agreed that Drew spoke the most truth on the matter and so they packed up and burned their wooden lodges and went south with Abraham helping them. Joyously Abraham knew that every day he got closer to Arkansas, he was closer to his home.

Chapter XXXI

A Journey South

Not all of the families moved with the tribe. Some dressed like the whites, spoke English like the whites, and used only English names. They wanted to blend in. But not the Naves. They went, like the others, south to the Arkansas territory.

Drew lent Abraham a horse and showed him much about the country as they traveled.

"That bitter nut Hickory there, you can make some good hickory balls out of that and keep them for a long time and then boil them when you want to eat 'em."

Abraham was smiling as he said this, "Drew, where were you before you came out here and became a Cherokee Indian?"

"I was a cotton Negro in Louisiana," Drew said, "But my master was a powerfully evil man. Once, after a whipping, I lit out, found my way to the river, and was taken by a group of Cherokees and I've been with them ever since. Fifteen years now," he said.

"Here," he said as he handed Abraham a rifle, "Now that we're on the move here, I gots to teach you how to shoot like a real frontiersman, and not no Georgia farmer."

Although Abraham had never had to hunt much for food, he learned much from Drew about how to come down wind on a deer and where to find possum and how to shoot grouse and wild turkey.

They crossed three rivers. The Cherokee traveled faster than Abraham thought a group of women and children could.

Unlike the last time they rode, this time Florence said little. But occasionally, when he would look in her direction, he could see that she had been looking at him.

It was heading toward winter, but by his calculations, Abraham could be back in the early spring, if he could get these people to let him go as soon as winter ended in their new land in Arkansas. He hoped desperately that the paddy-rollers had not come back and taken his own family, too. The thought had crossed his mind on many nights in his log cabin.

Chapter XXXII

Wado

The tribe was now deep in the northern part of Arkansas along the Chute River. The council had decided that this would be a good place to settle in the areas the government had said could be Indian. When they stopped working that evening after cutting down trees and eating the venison that Drew had shot, Abraham approached John Nave to talk about when he could leave.

"I think, Mr. Nave, that I've done all that has been asked of me, and I wonder if this is not a good time for me to be leaving."

Without looking at him, Nave simply said, "If you are to leave, then go. But do not leave without seeing my daughter. For she found you and she should be the last to say good-bye."

"Thank you again," Abraham said, "for saving me."

"We say 'wado'," Nave said.

"Then it is wado," said Abraham.

Abraham turned and walked away as he said this and found Drew to let him know that he was going to be leaving.

He returned to his sleeping place and began to gather his things for the long journey home in the morning. Florence was walking towards him with a bundle in her arms.

Abraham spoke first. "Florence. Your father says that my work is done and I can go, so I am coming to tell you."

She looked up at him, "I know," she said, "I knew you

127

would leave. I hoped that you were lying and you had no woman, and I thought maybe the longer you stayed, the more that you would want to stay." Then she held him tightly.

"I'm sorry," Abraham said, "but it's time."

It was harder than he thought to say these words to her. They had been together for months. Florence's voice and walk and the way she cared for him were deep in Abraham's mind. If he didn't leave now he knew he might never go.

With both hands, she pushed a package towards him and bowed her head.

"Here," she said, "This is for you. I made it for you because I thought that if we ever, if we ever . . ."

She slowly helped pull the old shirt off of Abraham. It was ragged and torn. Then she put over him the shirt that she had stitched for him and dyed in the colors of her people. In the cradle of the night, they laid together, neither thinking of tomorrow, nor who they were, nor where they came from, or where they were going. Thinking only of each other. Abraham forgot himself for the night and all the troubles he'd had. For them there was no tomorrow and they stayed as one in the night.

Abraham and Florence rose together in the morning knowing this was the time he had to go. Abraham, with the red shirt dyed by the red mulberry bark from Florence's own hard work, tucked the shirt into his pants and said to her, "Florence, what you have done for me is . . ."

"What is that," she said. "This shirt?"

"No," he said, "Everything."

"Why do they call you 'Comes-With-A-Feather'," he asked suddenly.

"Because my black hair stuck straight up on my head when I came out of my mother. The old woman who helped in the birthing laughed when she saw me and called out that I 'came with a feather.' So that is my name."

Abraham laughed out loud and she laughed too. It broke the awkwardness of their standing next to each other. Then they hugged as the morning sun rose upon the valley where her tribe had set themselves.

"You know I want you to stay," she said, "to be my man."

"I know," Abraham said, "I want to as well, but I must return. It pulls me back, as you must know."

"That is what makes me want you, too," she said.

He bent over and kissed her on the head.

"Wado," Abraham said.

Florence bowed her head, but would not look up. Then he straightened up and took one last look at her, waived good-bye, and went to Drew, who had a horse saddled.

As he rode away, he shouted out so the whole world would know, "I will wear this shirt proudly!" he said to her, "For Florence-Comes-With-A-Feather has made it for me. She who saved me from the river, then raised me up and gave me new life. Good luck to you, Florence!" he waived as he said this.

She looked up and waved back to him and said, "I shall see you some time when the trading's good."
The fingers of their hands waived good-bye in unison, to the beating of one heart to the turning of one world.

"Yes," she said finally crying to him as she waved, "When the trading is good."

And there upon his horse, Abraham rode northwest as fast as he could. Thinking slowly in his own mind of what he'd gained and lost, but also knowing that he finally was going back. Finally, to his home.

Chapter XXXIII

The Bitter Root

The passenger list of the Borialis out of Bantry Bay listed 30 passengers, but Edward Thornton knew better. He had buried his son, Stanton, alright, but found out within hours that it was Hoggen who struck the blow that killed his son. From that moment on, getting the Irishman was all he thought about. Though these Irish were a secretive bunch, as Thornton had found out in his years in dealing with them, he knew that a few schillings here and there or a drink or two would open a mouth to tell you what you needed to know. There was a 31st passenger on the ship. The livery driver remembered seeing an old woman kissing her son good-bye and waving him off as the ship departed. The liveryman described the woman exactly like Molly Hoggen.

Edward Thornton was not a man who would forget and the bitterness of the loss of his child, his son and heir to what he had achieved and built on this treeless land in Ireland was a deep and bitter root in his soul.

And so his neighbors, the Goodwyn's, were not surprised when he rounded up the local thugs and took the warrant from the Constabulary for Hoggen's arrest for murder and sailed to America to find Hoggen and bring him to justice. It might take years, but Thornton would find him.

Michael Greene and Frank Lynch didn't know Hoggen, but they knew good pay and were tough, strong men who knew how to squeeze information in almost any circumstance.

"I know why we're here," Greene said one day to Frank on the ship, "but what's he doing here? I thought Sweeney was a friend of Hoggen's."

"Yes, Sweeney, so why are you here?" Lynch poured out to him.

"I'm here for the money, like you. And I'm here to make sure you two and whoever else you hire don't kill Hoggen before he gets a trial. That's why I'm here."

Thornton gazed westward out on the deck, wishing his life coulda been like other peoples. His friends all had sons who were married and had grandchildren. All now taken from him by a stable boy he brought home and taught to be a horseman.

"It's a bitter pill," he said to Sweeney. "Like Cane and Abel, that this should be done by one whom I treated so well. But I will make him pay, as God is my judge, I'll make him pay."

While it was easy sailing to New Orleans, once Thornton got there, it was more difficult getting any information. The Irish came in hordes to work and they stuck together. They worked the swamps and didn't get as sick as the other laborers. So it took a few months before Frank Lynch was able to find out about a thin Irishman who loved to hang out at the horse track and who sounded an awful lot like Hoggen. It took another month before a horse tradesman was found who said that he had hired Hoggen to go up north and break horses for him for the Sante Fe Trail. The man said the Irishman never showed up.

"That's got to be him," Thornton said. "I knew he wouldn't find work on these canals or in the swamps. He's not a laborer like that. I knew if we looked for the horses, we'd find him. Damn him."

"We'll need more help than what we have," Sweeney said.

"We don't know this country. We've got to hire some men to go north."

And so Thornton's clan grew by ten and for sure they were a bric-a-brac crew as any can be bought in bars and outside of jails. A Creole, a Seminole Indian, two more Irish laborers, and five low-lives who each had a gun and a horse and would work for day wage. Thornton also posted wanted signs and sent them up the river with the porters to post at every port. There was no stopping the fury of his revenge and no cost that he wouldn't pay to get it.

Chapter XXXIV

Toward the River

A braham kept his red shirt tucked neatly in his trousers. He rode west eating his corn meal and salty dried jerky that Drew had given him. When he shot a raccoon, he dressed it and cooked it for his first hot meal in a week. He thanked Drew for teaching him how, and as he had learned from the Cherokee, he thanked the raccoon for giving his life so that Abraham could eat it.

In the many months since he had been gone, Abraham learned a lot about this land and he was different because of it. He looked different, too. His jaw had never healed exactly right and now, though his face was not so swollen, the right side of his jaw was stuck out a bit at an angle and he was thinner. Much thinner. His hair was grayer on the crown of his head, it was also receding, so he brushed it back to take the curl and stretched it straight back.

Goin' home, Abraham crossed rivers. He crossed the Cache River, the St. Francis River, all heading toward the Mississippi. He also knew he'd have to find some kind of work to pay for the ride north.

He met a man at Bear Creek Lake who took him south to a point where the river boats came and stopped. Earl Winn had a small livery stable and Abraham got work shoeing horses. At the docks where the riverboats came, he asked Sherwood Burns about the cost of passage north.

"Well, if you're travelin' first class, it's no cost to you at all, because we won't let no negroes ride there," he giggled, "but for as far as your going, it's going to be $15.

Abraham couldn't believe how much the man charged, but knowing how much he didn't have in his pocket, he said no more and went back to work.

"What's the signs there say," Abraham asked pointing at a poster next to the wall at the ticket counter.

"Oh, that's some blame Irishman wanted for murdering some Englishman. These things are getting plastered all up and down the river. It seems if you are an English lord, you can pretty near do anything. At least it says here that you get a reward of $1,000 from this English lord if you find this guy."

"Um," said Abraham, "seems like someone's always chasin' somebody, don't it."

"Seems that way to me," Burns said. "Anyways, if you see this guy Hoggen, you can make yourself $1,000 if you turn him in to Sir Edward Thornton," and Burns lifted his head up high mocking the look of an English gentleman as he said this.

"All I want is a way home," Abraham said. "I don't want no trouble from no one about nothin'."

That night the Northern Star stopped to let off folks at the docks. Looking out on the water, Edward Thornton spat his cigar into the Mississippi and watched as his cronies went out to ask the locals if they had seen or heard of an Irishman named Hoggen. Of course, the ticketman laughed and said he hadn't, but wished him good luck and told them they ought to come back anytime. Then away the boat went with Thornton's gang on it.

Abraham watched the lights of the Northern Star as it went up the great river. He wished he had the money to get on her. He hoped that another boat would come in a week's time and he had enough money to buy his way home.

Chapter XXXV

The Stand-Off

Hoggen was back to Sarah's farm the next day and trailing behind was the white starred ghost horse. When Hoggen arrived, Sarah didn't look at the horse as much as look at what wasn't on Hoggen's saddle bags.

"You're back sooner than I thought," she said. "Where's our supplies?"

"Well, it kinda started out like this. Ya see, I found this horse, corralled her, saved Gabe Owen's stock from being stolen by this she-devil and now I'm bringing her back because she's beautiful stock and I think if she can be broken, it would be the start of a whole new business on this farm. We could raise horses."

"What do you mean 'we'?" Sarah said. "All I did was ask you to go get me some supplies. Now you come back and you want to run a horse ranch and you got no supplies." Sarah turned and looked over the horse. "Is she even a rideable horse?"

"Well, she once was. I can tell, " Hoggen said. "And she will be again, I promise you."

"When are you going to get my supplies?"

"Sarah, give me a couple of days. Let me see what I can do with this horse, here, and then I'll take Judy down. I promise you."

Sarah sighed in resignation, "What do you call her?"

"I call her Ghost. She's the wild horse you've heard about."

135

"She's the what?" Sarah said. "There is no ghost . . "

"Oh, yes, there is. She's the one Rene was tellin' you about when he was up with Doc. They won't be seein' anymore livestock stolen. Not with her safely in your corral."

"Well, you listen to me. She better not break out of here and take our Judy with her."

Just then Reena came to the porch. "Mister Hoggen is that you? Well, glory be, you sure got back fast from the trading post."

"Well, actually, Miss Reena, I haven't gone there yet, but I've brought back this most gorgeous horse."

"Um, well, I guess we won't be eatin' that bacon for dinner that you didn't bring back, then," she said, and turned and slammed the door.

Hoggen put the great mare in the corral by herself and tied Judy up. He did not want to put her in with the Ghost until he started to work with her.

He watered her, gave her feed and then harnessed her to trot her around with on a lead rope. At every turn around the corral, Hoggen was more impressed with her. He talked to her constantly and when she came close to him, he'd drop her a crab apple. Still he couldn't touch her. It was as if she knew that he was trying to slowly entice her into trusting the Irish master who would soon try and ride her.

Meanwhile, Samuel stood between the railings and watched in silence. When Hoggen was finished, Samuel was at his feet.

"Mister Hoggen is that the ghost horse? How'd you catch her?"

"I snuck up on her, threw a rope around her and caught her like you would one of the little people in Ireland, except she isn't a pot of gold. Not yet. Not until I break her and maybe someday, I'll raise her foals."

"What a foal?" Samuel said.

"It's a little horse, a wee baby horse. I'll tell you what, maybe someday you'll have one of hers and you'll race her as fast as you can through the prairie like the wind, huh? What do you say, Samuel?"

"Yeah, a horse for me. You gonna teach me to read some more tonight?"

"Oh, yes, we will. Luke, Chapter 6, was always one of my favorites. That's the Sermon on the Mount."

Reena overheard them, and said out loud, "Oh, I love that one. Preacher used to say, 'Do not judge and you shall not be judged. Do not condemn and you shall not be condemned. Forgive and you shall be forgiven. Give and it shall be given unto you.' That's it, isn't it?"

"Aye, likely it is, Miss Reena. I think it says, 'For what you measure, it shall be measured to you.'"

"Yes, I'm sure it do," Reena said, "and the Lord's word is spoken true.

That night they read the Bible and Samuel was breaking out and smiling as Hoggen helped him read his words.

Sarah said to no one in particular, "I'm takin' Judy tomorrow to the trading post and getting the supplies myself, Hoggen. There is nothing to be done here for a couple of days that I can't go down and I could use the visit."

"Well, don't you worry about a thing. Everything will be fine here," he said, "don't you worry."

"It seems like every time a man tells me not to worry," Sarah said, "that's when I start."

The next morning Samuel said he wasn't feelin' good and Sarah decided not to go to the post, but to see if maybe he would get better before she left.

137

In the meantime, Hoggen was in the corral with The Ghost. As patient as Hoggen was with the horse, it was clear that they were in a stand-off. She wouldn't let Hoggen throw a blanket on her back. And try as he might, he couldn't get a bit in her mouth.

In the afternoon, he went to see how Samuel was doing. He sat down next to the boy who was laying in his bed.

"How you feelin', boy?"

"My joints aches all over," said Samuel. "How's the big Ghost Horse? Did you break her yet?"

"Not yet," said Hoggen, "but she'll come along nicely, I think."

"Can you tell me some more stories? Willy wants you to tell him about the kings in Ireland and wars with them Vikings."

"All in time, Samuel."

Suddenly Samuel asked, "Mr. Hoggen, is you poor?"

"Yes, Samuel, sadly I am. But you know I can read and write and no man who can read and write is really poor."

At that, Hoggen bent over the little boy and placed his hand on his chest. "A man can read and write, Samuel, is rich in here," he said, tapping the boy's chest. And then he pointed at his head, "And rich there, too. Once a man can read and write, Samuel, no chain will ever keep him. Some day, that's what will free Ireland and that's what will change your country too and what your folks have to live with."

Samuel looked up. "You mean slavery?"

"Yes, I do."

"I hate them all," Samuel said, "I hate them all. They killed my Daddy and Mama said they no good."

He patted the little boy's hand.

"That's me lad, Samuel," said Hoggen, "You be the defiant one, but use your mind as through your heart, lad. That's the best way. I see it in ya too, just like your Mama does. That's why she wants me to teach you how to read and write."

"I'm still not feelin' good," Samuel said. "Maybe I should take a little sleep now."

He yawned and Hoggen put the blankets up higher, and as he was dozing off to sleep, he said, "Mr. Hoggen, you got a little boy, too?"

"No," said Hoggen, "No, little boys. But if I did, I'd want him to be like you, little one. Just like you." And the boy went off to sleep and Hoggen went back out to the corral to see the ghost.

Chapter XXXVI

The Fever

Samuel kept getting worse. His joints were swelling and rashes were all over his body. But try as they might, Reena and Sarah couldn't get the boy's condition to turn.

In the candlelight that night, an exhausted Sarah said to Reena, "Mama Reena, what are we going to do? The boy's ankles and knees and elbows is all swollen up and he's just in powerful pain."

"I can't say, 'cept I know that the boy has a strong spirit and I hope to God he'll come through this," Reena said.

"I'll just die," said Sarah, "if that boy gets any worse. Mama Reena, I just can't stand it no more, I can't."
Hoggen came in quietly to see how Samuel was and to say good night. When he overheard their talking, he asked, "What about Doc? The Indian medicine man that was with Rene. Perhaps he can help. If you like, I'll go in the morning."

Reena blurted out, "Sure can't hurt, Mr. Hoggen, just tell him about the swellin' and the fever and the rashes, and God's speed to ya."

That night a rain came and the lightening flashed strips of bright light that Hoggen saw through the cracks in the walls of the barn where he was sleeping. He brought in Judy and The Ghost, and together the three listened to the rain pounding on the roof. All the while, Hoggen realized that the mud would slow his way to Rene's trading post.

"Damn bad luck," he said to himself, "but Judy will have to go and give it her best tomorrow.

When the morning came, the sky was bright blue and clear and Hoggen set off.

"Come on, now, Judy, with luck we can get there and back by tomorrow morning. Come along now, missy," he said as he heeled into her sides to get her to gallop a little before they got to the deep grasses.

But as he was riding her, he felt her favoring her left fore-leg, and after a mile or so, got off to see what was her trouble.

"Come on, now Judy, you can't be doing this now."

He touched her shoulders and didn't feel any heat. He pressed against her for some tenderness. He walked her some more and she was still limping even when he wasn't on her, and when he looked at her hoof, he realized what was wrong.

"She's got the thrush," he said as he touched the tender frog between her hoof. "Lord, Judy, how did you get this? It's my fault, not tending to you."

With that, he brought the limping horse back and as the sun was rising over the small farm, he had to tell Sarah the bad news.

"I'm sorry, Sarah, Judy's lame, we can't do anything right now."

Sarah simply buried her face in her hands and cried, and Hoggen stood there watching, feeling a failure that he couldn't help the little boy or his Mama.

He spent the rest of the day tending to Judy, but by early nightfall, he had brought the Ghost out.

"Come on, girl, if ever there's a time for us to do it, let's do it now."

At that, he put the bit in her mouth and tried to place a blan-

141

ket and saddle on her. Little Willy watched as Hoggen jumped on the horse and was promptly thrown off.

"Damn you, you Ghost," he said, wishing he hadn't sworn in front of the little boy. "Can't you see I need your help."

But the horse simply shook her mane and tromped off, away. It was a long night that night, with Sarah and Reena putting compresses on the boy and giving him Jerusalem tea to break the fever. They could hear the Ghost horse occasionally sending out her call for the stallion she still missed.

Chapter XXXVII

Jude's Eye

It was Boyle who saw him first. He and Libbing had gone to Earl Wyn's to talk about purchasing a wagon for their business up in Missouri now that they had gotten bounty off the previous summer's catches. Abraham was shoeing a chestnut mare and had turned to get another shoe. Boyle who, as usual was not listening to Libbing speaking with Earl Wyn, recognized the face.

As they were leaving, Boyle leapt to Libbing's ear.

"Did you see that Nigger? Did you see him? That's the one that got Watson! He didn't drown! He must have floated down here and he's working at Wyn's livery.

"What?" said Libbing, "let me go around and see."

At that point, Libbing and Boyle walked lightly around and looking into the huge doors of livery, saw Abraham working on the same chestnut horse.

"That's him, sure enough," Boyle said.

"But don't startle him," Libbing said, "it's time we get the law involved." And off they went to the sheriff to swear out a warrant.

Before finishing his work that day, Mr. Wyn came up and complimented Abraham on his fine work.

"Abraham, I sure enjoy the work you're doing here. You got a job here as long as you like."

"Sir, I'm trying to get back to my family."

"Where are they?" asked Mr. Wyn.

"Up north near Arrow Rock, what they used to call New Philadelphia."

"Well, that's a ways up."

"Also, Mr. Wyn, could I ask ya to maybe writes a letter to one of my friends, Rene, who is running a trading post up there, to let him know I'm all right. You see, I had an accident some time ago, and they think I might be dead or something."

"What?" said Wyn, asking Abraham directly.

Abraham felt in his heart it would be okay to tell the man his long story. Little did he know that the timing of it was such that the sheriff was coming just as Wyn listened intently. As he knocked on the door, the sheriff yelled out to Mr. Wyn.

"Mr. Wyn, I got business with that negro in there, now, you bring him on out."

Behind the sheriff stood Boyle and Libbing smiling like they'd just won a prize at a county fair.

Before anything could be said, the sheriff put shackles on Abraham and took him off.

"What's he arrested for?"

"Murder," said the sheriff, "These here fellows have sworn out a warrant saying he killed a fellow by the name of Watson. He's an escaped slave, too."

"I ain't no escaped slave," said Abraham, "That's what started this whole ruckus, now. I'm a free man, I tell ya.

"Well, free or not, you're here for murder, and the circuit judge comin' in a day or so. Then we'll find out then what's what."

Abraham thought quick. As he was being led away, he yelled out to Mr. Wyn, "Mister Wyn, you gots to help me. Send that letter up for Rene. His name is . . . "

But before he could say anything else, the sheriff hauled him off. Wyn was an honest white man and he believed Abraham's story. He went to go see Jude Garavogue, a lawyer and a saloon owner.

Jude Garavogue had one bright hazel colored eye and a black patch over the other. The patch looked kinda funny as it perfectly matched the black vest and black coat he was always wearing around his stout body. All this black was topped off with his pure white hair. Folks said that Jude only needed the one good eye because its light pale greenish brown color seemed to look right through people.

"You sure have taken a liking to this black fellow only working a couple of days for ya," he said to Wyn when Wyn told him the story of Abraham's escape.

"Look here, not all of us is slavers."

"If I didn't know better," Jude said as his one eye twinkled, "I'd say you're an abolitionist."

"Shush," Wyn said, "Don't use those words around here. You know what it's like here in Missouri."

"Well calm yourself," Jude said, "I'll go talk to this Abraham and sees what I can do."

"You know he won't have no money."

Jude looked at Mr. Wyn, "Somehow, Mr. Wyn, good causes ain't never about money, anyway."

Jude Garavogue was the type of man that didn't always please people, but owning the best saloon in town where everyone came to quench their thirst, gave him a kind of independence that other men envied.

Abraham was being kept in a stinking cell next to the livery stables. Jude cleared his throat as he walked in and saw a black man hunched in a corner.

"They tell me you killed a paddy-roller by the name of Watson. They also tell me you a free man and ain't no runaway slave. Is that true?"

Abraham looked up and eyed the man standing there, "As God is my judge, sir, it's true. But who, may I ask, is you?"

"My name is Jude. Jude Garavogue, and if you let me, I think I might be of some assistance to get you out of this here predicament."

At that, he held out his hand. Abraham stood up and shook it and looked up and said, "How can you help me, there, Mr. Jude?"

"Well, I'm a lawyer as well as a saloon keeper, and never should two professions have ever been a match as them two. Now, tell me what happened," Jude said, as he pulled out a quill pen and ink blotter and a scratch parchment.

"Where should I begin?" Abraham said.

"I've found it best to always start at the beginning."

It didn't take Jude long to realize that what Abraham need-ed most was witnesses and some kind of affidavit, if he could get one, from attorney Stein. However, it would take too long to get the affidavit from Stein, and therefore, Jude sent a letter up to Rene at the trading post to come down and to bring the ferry-man with him who he knew witnessed what had happened.

"Please, Mr. Jude, if you could send something for my wife to let her know I'm alive."

"I'll place something in my letter to Rene and get it on today's riverboat, but we have to hurry. As I told ya, the judge comes next Tuesday, and we better be prepared."

"I trust ya, Mister, I know you'll do right."

"Yes, that's what I'll do, alright," said Jude, "but now I have to get back to my saloon and drop this down at the steamboat quay."

Abraham had been in some fixes before, but he sure hoped this one eyed lawyer could get him out of this one. He chuckled to himself in disgust when he thought of making peace with the dead man as he thought he had done with the Cherokee Tucker Grayson.

"Some peace," he thought.

The night was long and he slept fitfully.

Chapter XXXVIII

She Rides The Wind

Hoggen was angry. Angry at himself and blaming himself for Judy's lameness. Mostly he was angry at the heavens for making the little boy sick, and frustrated that nothing could be done unless they could get to Doc and perhaps he could give the boy something. The night sky was sparkle clear. The stars and the moon put a whitish glow on the ground. Although he tried and failed so many times, Hoggen was determined that the stand-off between he and the ghost would end that night.

He was a man possessed. He wrapped rags dipped in pitch on wood stakes, then tied them to the corral posts and lit the rags on fire, making a circular fire around the corral, it looked like a huge birthday cake. He brought the ghost out, and although it was night, fed her crab apple, and talked to her soothingly.

"You must do this for me, you must! The boy will die if we don't get help. I know you have it in ya. Come on, now. There's the girl. There's the girl," he soothed.

Then, jumping on her, the black mare bucked, and bucked some more. The commotion startled Sarah, who came out and watched.

"You're going to wake everybody trying break that fool horse," Sarah said, "Go to bed, Hoggen."

"No, not . . . until . . . I've . . . done it!" he yelled in such a stern voice that it took Sarah back as she didn't know the man could echo such a strong response. He gripped and held on tighter than ever before. Time after time she'd buck him off, and then he'd get back on. Finally, after twirling and spinning in the yellow light of the torches, the horse stopped bucking. This time she would submit . . . to him. He threw his arms around her thick muscled neck, and patting her, told Sarah, "Open the gate, we're goin' to see the Doc."

Without a word, Sarah opened the gate, and the Ghost was trotting around the fire ring of the corral one more time with her white star shinning on her black forehead. Then Hoggen took off on the Ghost. The moon illuminated the ground and he whis-tled an old song he'd remembered from his days in Ireland and talked to the horse as they rode along.

"I knew you'd come around to me. I knew you would. You'll save the lad, I tell you, you will. There's my girl."

In the dawn, Hoggen saw the high grass yield to a low lying fields. At that, Hoggen let her run to see what she could do. He remembered seeing her run from a distance, but now, on her, the power she had, the gait, she just gobbled up the ground as she ran to the ferry landing. The wind tugged at Hoggen's cheeks and chilled his nose and her breathing and snorting were in rhythm with her gallop.

"She rides like the wind," he said to himself, and when he got to the ferry crossing, he hot walked her until the ferrymen arrived.

"You're here early. I was even going to have a bit of coffee, but I saw you from across the river. I saw that horse moving! What a gait!"

"Sarah Cooper's boy's sick. I have to see if Doc can help," Hoggen said urgently, "Can you hurry me across?"

"Aye, I can."

And the ferryman and his two workers pulled across as fast as they could.

"As soon as I can get something, I'll be back," said Hoggen to the ferryman.

"I don't expect I'll see ya back for a while."

"I'll be back, don't you worry," he said.

Rested again, Hoggen put the mare in a full gallop all the way to the trading post. Beads of frothy sweat were rolling down her broad, black chest when Hoggen ran into Rene.

"Where's Doc, Rene? Samuel's so sick!"

"He's back in the shed," Rene said.

Without any more words, Hoggen ran back to see Doc. He pounded on the door and the old Indian opened it.

"Sarah's boy is sick and needs your help, Doc."

The old Indian bade him come in and Hoggen sat down, looking around at the inside of the shed which was filled with bottles and in the bottles all kinds of different plants and dead animals.

"Tell me what you've seen," said Doc.

Hoggen explained about the rash and all the joints hurtin' and the swellin' and Doc shook his head without saying anything.

"Here," he said, "this root will help. Boil it. Make tea. He must chew this moss and get a mouth full of saliva, chew some more and swallow."

Hoggen nodded and took the package of roots and moss and was running back to Rene's trading post when he saw a poster outside Dicey Morgan's saloon. His mouth dropped. There was his name and a reward. His breath was tight and he didn't know what to say. Behind him, the big Frenchman came up.

"I did not have time to tell you, Hoggen. I've pulled down three of those. A very determined man is after you. If I were you, I would not come back here again."

Hoggen nodded his head, "It will never end. Rene, I'm off now. I may not see you again."

"Perhaps not, my friend, but you ride well and long."

Within hours, Hoggen was back on the ferry, then across the Missouri, galloping the Ghost. As he rode, all he could think of was Thornton. That and the Ghost. It was the way she moved so effortlessly. Then he thought of her in the wild. He had snatched her back and now someone wanted to snatch him back, too, he thought. "How funny – seems like we can't ever leave things free.

He had run this horse farther and faster than you should ride a horse, but he had to get back as soon as he could. Then, after a ride that would kill most horses, he arrived back at the cabin. Sarah threw her arms around him to thank him, but he was so exhausted after that, he didn't even wait to see how Sarah and Reena did with giving the boy his root tea and moss.

He fed and bedded down the Ghost and collapsed to sleep in the barn.

The next morning, he went to the cabin early, "How's the little boy? How's Samuel?"

"He's much better this mornin'," Reena said. "Must have been something in the root that killed the fever and reduced the swellin'. He'll be up and around in a few days for sure."

"That's good," Hoggen said, much relieved. "Listen, Miss Reena, I have to talk to ya about something, now," said Hoggen.

"What's that?" said Mama Reena.

"I saw a poster of me down by the trading post. The man I told ya about, he's here in America and he's huntin' for me."

"Well, we'll hide ya good. They won't find ya here."

"I shouldn't stay too much longer, but I worry about all of

you."

"No you gotta stay, Mister Hoggen, they won't find ya here. Please, just stay."

"They'll find me, Reena, and maybe hurt you. I can't let them do that now."

"Oh, but I gonna miss you, Hoggen. I surely will," Reena said in a sad voice.

"And I you," said Hoggen, "and I you."

"Say nothing to Sarah right now, please Mr. Hoggen. I'll tell her when it's right." Reena said in a whisper of a voice.

Chapter XXXIX

Thompson's Dance

With Samuel feeling better, it was as if a great sigh of relief blew around the house. People's shoulders dropped as tension ran from them. Smiles came up watching the little boy get better and better.

Every Fall, the Thompsons would send word around to all that it was time to have a big feed at their house to kinda celebrate the ending of the harvest time. It didn't much matter to Ella Thompson if you was new to the community or old, so long as you showed up and either brought some food with you, or a song, or if Mr. Thompson had his say, some corn liquor.

Mama Reena was rocking and knitting on the porch and when the door creaked, she turned without even questioning who it was, and said "Sarah, you know the Thompson's dance is coming up. 'Bout time we went back to it."

"Mama Reena, I don't feel like dancing much. Besides, I haven't been there since . . ."

Before she could finish the sentence, Reena said, "I know. Since Abraham. But you can't hold these children up from seeing other people. They need to go out and be with other youngins, too. Get a feel for the sound of folks laughin' and dancin' and carryin' on. I'm fixin' to make some syrup and cornbread cakes, and if you can get that Mr. Hoggen man out of the corral with that black mare of his, I bet he'd like to come, too."

Sarah really didn't want to go. She didn't have no need for

dancing, but Mama Reena was right. And besides, she missed seeing folk. She walked over to the corral. Hoggen stood there with the Ghost, and she watched him stroke the mare gently with his long fingers.

"Hoggen, you're gonna spoil that horse, you know. She'll never be good for plowin'."

"Aye, but I could shoe her with golden horseshoes for savin' little Samuel!"

"Mr. Hoggen, the Thompsons, you know the Thompsons? The folk I told you about? They're havin' a bit of a git together and seein' as how I know you like to talk about your days back in the Ireland country, I'm sure they would like to have you come along with us and pull you a bit on those stories."

"A party, you say? Oh, I'll be there! None likes a good time like the Irish. I'm a fair dancer, you know, too. I once took first place at the Turran Strand Festival!"

At which point Sarah watched in amazement as the lanky Irishman stood up and started kicking his heels to and fro, slapping his feet back and forth with the ground like she had never seen before.

"Well, ah, well, Hoggen, ah, we don't dance that way," she said. "And I'm not so sure that the folks here are ready . . , I mean know, your dances. Ah, it may not mix real well."

"I could teach the boys, too!"

"No, no, that will be alright, now, I'm sure."

"No, I'm going to teach 'em for sure. We could do a three-handed jig, ya know, and . . ."

"Mr. Hoggen, please, I'm sure we will all be happy to have you come, but ain't no need to teach the boys."

That next afternoon, everyone picked up their sleeping blankets and rolled them and put them in the wagon. They hitched up Judy who was still favoring her leg a bit, but was good enough to travel, and off the family went with Hoggen trailing behind on the Ghost. As they reached the crest of the last hill and could see below, a big fire pit was burning and the soft trill sounds of a fiddle and a banjo could be heard lazily playing in the pale light of the early evening. Even Judy seemed to perk her ears and trot faster to get down to the party.

As big as he was, Mr. Bolling sang in a high tenor voice and got the whole crowd a roaring around him as he sang for folks.

Sarah was leaning against the wagon with the fire throwing yellow tongues of light upon her face when Hoggen suddenly jumped in front of her.

"Miss Sarah, it would do these legs of mine a lot of good if you'd come and dance a bit with me."

"Hoggen, thank you, but please . . ."

As his blue eyes looked directly into hers, Hoggen said, "Aye . . . come now." He grabbed her hand and dragged her onto the dirt area in front of the fire pit while the band was playing a quick footed reel. Mr. Bolling was singing in his high tenor voice:

> "And when she goes,
> she goes this way,
> and them that goes,
> will spin this way,
> then bring her again,
> into your arms, and
> spin away, spin away
> spin away yarns."

And each time he said "way" he'd point his arms and the whole group would have to go in the direction that he would point.

Despite herself, Sarah enjoyed the dance with Hoggen and never realized he could dance this well. The easiest she had ever been with. She didn't even realize she was laughing out loud as he spun her around. Then the whole group, exhausted from Bolling's calls and chants to go back and forth, broke up. Hoggen and Sarah hugged each other, out of breath from all the dancing, and Hoggen was still looking at her with a huge grin on his face. He was breathing hard and she was too, and their eyes just locked on each other. For a moment, Sarah forgot all the bad, all the hard times, and for the first time in a very long while, she felt safe and happy gazing into the laughing Irishman's glittering eyes.

Mrs. Thompson came up from behind, "My goodness you too was a crackin' the acorns on that floor. Goodness, gracious, how 'bout some lemonade to quench that thirst of yours, Mr. Hoggen?" Mrs. Thompson said as she put her arm under his and walked him over to a table where there was some lemonade that Mrs. Thompson knew her husband had spiked with a bit of the old "tin jitter" as she used to say. Of course, standing around it was all the gentlemen who had just pranced around the floor with their women. As she was walking away, Mrs. Thompson turned and winked her eye at Sarah and nodded, making Sarah blush that someone else had noticed.

Chapter XL

Comes Rene

"Rene? Are you Rene?"

"Yes, I am," Rene said to the riverboat pilot of the *Belle Flower*.

"This is a letter urgent from a man by the name of Jude Garavogue, down south in Allen County."

"What would he want with me?" Rene said.

"About a man down there, I guess. Some kind of a murderer."

"I don't know of any murderers," Rene said in half questioning tone, but took the letter just the same and opened it up.

After he read the letter, Rene sat down and he exhaled his response, "Abraham's alive!"

He ran to Doc, "Doc, Abraham's alive! He's been arrested for murdering that "paddy-roller" and he's being tried down in Allen County! I have to go! Doc, can you take care of the trading post while I'm gone."

"I can, but you know I always sell cheaper to Indians!" he laughed.

"Oh, tell Sarah! Get word to Sarah that Abraham's alive. Doc, please."

"I'll send word," Doc replied, but said under his breath, "in time."

Garavogue had asked that Rene bring any documents or information or any witnesses. Rene knew of only one witness.

The ferryman. He rode up to the ferry landing to meet Joe Boreman.

"Joe, I've come to get you and take you down to save a life."

Boreman looked up, "Big Rene, how am I going to save a life today?"

"Because you saw Abraham struggle with that paddy-roller and can say it was in self-defense."

"He's alive? Where? Where is he? What's happened?"

"It is down in Allen County, and you must help."

"But I've got my ferry to run."

"Your boys can run it for a while. Come, there is a keel boat heading south. We've got to take it now."

"But, I've . . ."

Rene put both of his bear paw hands on the shoulders of Boreman and pushed him along and Joe barely had time to tell his two boys that he was going and what they needed to do to run the ferry across the river. He was hoping to tell Boreman's boys to send word on the next person crossing to Sarah to tell her that Abraham was alive, but in the excitement of it all, he plum forgot.

"First, we have to get Abraham out of jail," he said to himself. "That's what we need to do first."

Chapter XLI

The Candle

It was late in the evening. The time between the end of one day and the beginning of another. Sarah guarded the candle flame with her hand as she walked across the yard and into the barn. Only the candle light illuminated the room in a soft glow as she entered.

Hoggen lay in the hay and straw sleeping peacefully. Sarah cleared her throat a little, thinking that would wake him. When it didn't, she bent low with the candle and touched his chest.

"Hoggen," she said, "Mister Hoggen."

Hoggen's eyes opened and he looked up to see Sarah's face framed by the candle light.

"Something wrong? How's the . . . "

She put her fingers to his lips and said, "No."

Hoggen's arms slid around Sarah and gently pulled her to him before he even thought about it as Sarah's hand touched his face.

"Thank you," she said, "thank you for making me feel happy again."

No other words were spoken, just the candle and two souls holding each other and breathing as one. Breathing together as a man and a woman do. Each giving what the other needed, tenderly, carefully, slowly in a dance as old as time.

As first light of the morning showed through the barn door, there was a sharp rap of a stick on the barn door as Reena came barrelin' through.

"Sarah? Is you in there? Mister Hoggen?"

They were both startled and Hoggen jumped as he sat up. They rolled around and Reena could hear them putting on their clothes and breathing hard.

"Is you both in there?" Reena demanded.

"Yes, Mama Reena, we must have fallen asleep, and well. . ."

"Well, git up now, and don't be so scandalous. You got youngins in the house. Get a movin'." And she swung her stick and hit Sarah on the ankle.

"Ouch! Now stop that, Mama Reena!"

"Go on, get movin' now. Scandalous things!" And she laughed to herself as she said it.

Hoggen jumped up and pulled himself together, mumbling good morning, but Reena would have none of that.

"Come for breakfast when I call, and make sure your draws is up!" At that she laughed again and stick walked her way back to the house.

Chapter XLII

Thornton's Ride

Edward Thornton lit his cigar. He lit the cigar every time the riverboat would stop and he would send his cronies out to inquire as to the Irishman.

"I'll find him soon, my boy," he said to himself, "and take him back dead or alive.

One afternoon, Greene came running back up the gang plank shouting.

"Mister Thornton, Mister Thornton! Man here says the Irishman you're looking for was here last winter, heading north for a job for breakin' horses."

"I knew it!" said Thornton. "He doesn't even know we're coming. Pay the man five dollars and let's go."

He puffed even harder on his cigar as he thought about how he might be able to finally sleep once this work was done.

"Greene, you're doing a good job and you'll make a bonus when its done."

"Aye," said Sweeney, "a bonus. We'll all get a bonus to find an old friend."

"The money's good money," Thornton spat back, "and whether you came or not, it'd still be here and your old friend would still be a dead man."

"I'm not here to bring him back dead," Sweeney said, "We'll let him stand trial. That's what I'm here to make sure happens."

"As you say, but whatever happens, it'll be God's will and mine, too."

"Yes, Mr. Thornton," said Sweeney, "God's will for sure."

Rene and the ferryman didn't see who was on board the steamboat that blew its steam whistle at them as it headed north and they headed south. They couldn't warn Hoggen of what was comin' his way, but then again, they had their own fight to fight and it would be only a another full day's journey before they got there.

Chapter XLIII

Libbing's Fall

Jude met Rene at the saloon and listened to the story that the ferryman had to tell of what had happened.

"Do you have any document that show's that Abraham's a free man?"

"I did not have time to go up to his farm to find one, if it still exists, but I've got this contract that I sold him the farm and I've seen his papers," said Rene in a concerned voice, "can that be enough?"

"It's gonna have to be," said Jude, "The judge comes here tomorrow and Morton Curry is going to prosecute if the judge thinks there's enough evidence."

There was no court house for the circuit judge, only the bar which had to be cleared of all liquors. Chairs were drawn up for the jury, should there be one, when Judge William Cafferty, a long-eared, long-nosed man with little humor in his face, sat down.

"Well, gentlemen, this appears to be a rather clear case of murder by a run-away slave," said the Judge.

"Judge, if it would please ya to listen," said Jude, "I think there's some assumptions there that you're makin' that clearly are erroneous and without merit."

"Such as?" said the judge.

"Well, this Negro is a free man and there's papers documentin' it in Georgia, which we can get, if necessary."

"Well, the papers aren't here, are they?"

"No, sir. They was dislodged when this man was unlawfully hog tied by that man Libbing, there."

Libbing stood up, "I did no such thing!" And the judge banged his gavel.

"You sit down there. You're time will come to talk. And what other evidence do you have Mr. Garavogue?"

"I've got two witnesses, one of whom saw the altercation, and is prepared to say that even if the man did act in killin', it was done in self-defense."

Again, Libbing stood up.

"Self-defense! No, that nigger . . . "

"Sit down, sir, or I'll have you thrown out of this saloon . . . er, I mean courtroom."

A crowd of people from the town had gathered to see the event so that there was only standing room inside Even the overflow outside could be heard laughing at the judge's mistake.

"Well, I'm not wasting my time on a trial if there's no evidence worthy of putting the whole thing on. Mr. Prosecutor, what offer are you makin'?"

"The witness here is Mr. Libbing, a well-known and well thought of businessman and his employee, Mr. Boyle."

"Well, let's hear from Mr. Libbing, then."

And at that, the prosecutor put Mr. Libbing in a chair and had him tell his whole story, including how Abraham, unprovoked, strangled and killed Mr. Watson while trying to escape after he had been detained as a run-away.

"Wait, you're not done," said the judge when Libbing stood up after the prosecutor had finished. "Mr. Garavogue?"

"Thank you, your honor. Mr. Libbing, you're a paddy-roller, aren't you?"

"I don't consider myself a . . . "

"You take slaves and return them, do you not sir?"

"I do."

"And those would be run-away slaves, would they not?"

"They would."

"And this here colored fellow, this Nigra right here, he's a run-away slave?"

"He is."

"And how do you know it?"

"'Cause he's a Nigra!" and Libbing chuckled to himself at that.

"What did you say to him before you decided he was a run-away?"

"Hump! You don't say nuthin' to um. You jump on um and hits um and get paid for it when you brings um in."

"And what evidence do you have that he is a slave and that he ain't free?"

"None. Just like you ain't got none that he is free," Libbing said.

"The event on the ferry, as I understand your testimony, was an unprovoked attack. Is that right?"

"Unprovoked as ever. He just up and strangled my friend Watson and fell into the river and I thought they had both drown. And that's the truth."

"Where were you sitting on this ferry?"

"Why, I was sittin' right at the front, near the side goin' south to shore!"

Garavogue cocked his head, "Okay, and this was at about 3:00 in the afternoon, wasn't it?"

"Why, yes, it must have been," Libbing crowed.

"And I'm sure that you'd agree, Mr. Libbing, that the sun,

she sets in the west out here in Missouri."

"Why, I do believe you're correct, far as I know, it always sets that way."

"And so you was facin' west, then."

"Yes, I was," Libbing said. "Right directly so I could see what that nigra did to my man."

"And now, sir, if I'm correct, with the sun setting in the west at 3:00 o'clock in the afternoon, it would be settin' angulated into your face, so you had to shield your eyes, or you couldn't have even seen this commotion."

"I could, sir, 'cause I was wearin' my hat. I could see perfectly well." Old Libbing said, satisfied that he'd out smarted Jude.

"And was you wearin', what, the hat that you got in your hand there?"

"Yes, sir."

"That was all you was wearin', was the hat?"

"Yes, sir."

"You weren't wearin' nothing else, now were you?"

"No, I wasn't."

"Ya sure, now, nothing on your face or your head? Just that hat?"

"As God is my judge," Libbing crowed.

"And so if I step back, oh, about this far, sir," at which point Garavogue stepped back a good few paces, "You sees then, at least this far, could you not? This whole commotion, was about this far away, wasn't it?"

"I do believe that's correct, sir."

"Mr. Libbing, I would ask you to close your eyes for a minute."

"Objection, your honor!" said the prosecutor, "This seems

166

out of line and unorthodox and without any foundation whatso-
ever!"

"Overruled! Sit down, let's see what he's doing."

At that point Libbing closed his eyes and Jude Garavogue
brought two folks up from the crowd behind the chairs and put
them together, right where he was standing, with one man in the
arm of the other, like they was a tussling in a fight.

Garavogue said, "Now, boys," and he shushed down the
crowd when he said this, "you be quiet now, cause we have to
have Mr. Libbing, here, explain to us just exactly how he saw
this fight go down. So stand there, boys, just like I have you.
Don't move at all, now, don't move.

"Now, your honor, if you could, I'd like to have Mr. Libbing
up there put that hat on his head just like he did the day he saw
this and open up his eyes and show me what he seen."

At that, the Judge told Mr. Libbing to put the hat on his
head, and there standing some ways away was two people all
entangled like they were about to flail at each other real good.

"So, Mr. Libbing, are your eyes open?""Yes, they are."

"See these two fellas here?"

"Why sure I do, plain as day."

At that, the crowd murmured a bit.

"And is that the way they looked when your man there got
attacked by this here nigra?" Garavogue pointed at Abraham.

"Just like that! Just like that, I swear!"

"Well, who's a hittin' whom, here?"

"Huh?" Libbing said.

"Well, who's hitting whom?"

"I don't know what you mean by that," Libbing said.

"Well, the man on the left, who is that man?"

"I don't know who that man is. What do you mean 'who the
man is'?"

167

At that, the whole bar shook in laughter.

"Mr. Libbing," Mr. Garavogue said, "the man on the left is Boyle. He works for ya. And the man on the right is the dry goods salesman's wife, Ms. Jorgensen! She ain't no man at all!"

And at that the entire barroom burst into laughter and screams of delight.

"Mr. Libbing, have you ever worn glasses or focals of any type?"

At that, an angry Libbing turned bright red, stood up and burst out, "You high falutin' ain't trickin' me! I know what I seen, dammit! I know what I seen, dammit!" He was flailing his arms, and the judge, pounding his gavel, had two of the bigger ruffians in the bar haul him off the stand and out of the saloon. As he was being carried away, Mr. Garavogue turned to him and said out loud for all to hear, "No other questions."

Garavogue continued, "Your honor, before this proceeds to a full-blown trial, I'd like to have the testimony of the ferryman heard."

Rene and Abraham looked at each other, but couldn't talk. All Abraham could say without speaking out was, "THANK YOU, Rene."

"If it's necessary, put him on."

At which point Jude put the ferryman on the stand. He nodded in recognition of Abraham and Abraham nodded back.

"Yes, sir, there was three negroes on the wagon, including that man, Abraham."

"And how do you know him?"

"Well, he's been farmin' with his family up north away for some years."

"And was he a runaway slave?"

"Objection!" the prosecutor said.

"Overruled," said the judge.

"As far as you know, sir, was he?"

"No, sir, he was a free man far as I know. Told me about how he had done it and all. Bought his freedom, he did, from his master in Georgia."

"And when did you realize that this man, Abraham, was in the wagon of this paddy-roller, Mr. Libbing?"

"Tell you the truth, sir, I wasn't paying much attention until I seen that white man Watson up and hit old Abraham right in the jaw with the butt of his rifle. Then I realized who it was, but . . ."

"And was Mr. Abraham in chains at time, sir?"

"Yes, sir, he was."

"And what happened then?"

"Well, he put up his hands and they rolled and rolled right into the river, and I thought they both had drowned."

"And so it was you that seen Mr. Watson strike first, is that right sir?"

"Yes, it is."

"Was you wearing a hat that day, sir?"

"Yes, sir, as always."

"Do you wear spectacles?" Garavogue asked and the bar room erupted in laughter again.

"No, sir, never have."

Garavogue pointed to the other end of the bar, "What color shirt is that man wearing over there?"

"Dark blue, sir. Looks right dandy on him, too."

Again the bar erupted into laughter, and the judge pounded his gavel, "That will be enough of this frivolity!"

"Thank you. Your honor, I would like to move to have the charges brought by the prosecutor withdrawn as it's evident that

169

this was self-defense."

"Anything else to say, there?"

"No."

"Mr. Prosecutor?"

"It's clear that a run-away slave . . . "

"Sir, what evidence do you have that this man is a run-away slave?"

"Well, sir, there is no evidence that he isn't."

"What evidence do you have that he is?"

"None, other than he's a nigra."

"Well, then, stop using the term and tell me what evidence you have of an unprovoked act of murder on this Watson fellow?"

"Other than Mr. Libbing and his worker, Mr. Boyle, none sir."

"Dismissed. I can't foresee puttin' twelve good men in a seat to listen to this when it's clear to me that there is no evidence of anything other than an accident between a paddy-roller and what appears to be, at best, free negro, with no papers. But I will do this. I will inquire in the county of Georgia where this man claims that he is free and if it turns that this is not true, I will have this man back in chains in my courtroom. You understand that Abraham Cooper?

Abraham stood up astonished at what was going on.

"Yes, sir, I do. I do, sir."

"Good."

Jude stood up at that point. "Your honor, if this courtroom is no longer officially a courtroom, then I say the saloon is now open and drinks on the house for everyone, courtesy of Jude Garavogue!"

At that, the whole crowd in and outside Jude's saloon roared with approval and Rene slapped Abraham's back and whispered in his ear, "Let's get out of here before they change their mind."

Abraham shook Jude's hand, "I've got nothin' to pay, sir, but I will.

"Yes, I know you will. Mr. Jude Garavogue never takes a case for free. It will be twenty-five dollars gold and I'll charge you interest if you don't pay me in a year!" and at that, the man winked his one eye at Abraham and turned to catch the hand of the other man to shake it and then he grabbed a glass of whisky from the barman and the whole bar gave a cheer to Jude Garavogue, the best lawyer-saloon owner in all the West.

Chapter XLIV

Angels So Close

Sarah was cleaning up after making breakfast. Samuel's appetite was at full tilt and she was glad of it. She reached over, wiping her hands on her apron, and for the first time in a long while, picked up Abraham's fiddle and was just holding it thinking back fondly of her lost man. Reena, as always, burst through the door, her stick clacking on the first chair to the right and she felt it with her hands and sat down.

"Sarah, I didn't want to say it before, but Mr. Hoggen's got bad news."

Still in the day dream of her recollection of her man, Sarah looked up.

"What you mean, bad news?"

"There is a wanted poster for him. Rene showed it to him at the post when he went to get the medicine. He's gonna have to run for it some time soon. After last night, well, I thought you should know."

"What? Run for it? Are you sure, Mama Reena?"

"Sure as what he told me. Go talk to him."

"When did you know, mama Reena?"

"A while ago, but the time wasn't right to tell ya. But now it is."

"You had no right not to say something! No right at all!" and Sarah ran out the door.

Outside she saw Hoggen sitting on the top fence post of the

corral. The Ghost was prancing with her legs high, snorting the morning air.

Sarah was about to say something to Hoggen, but stopped. She could hear him singing softly and he was looking out past the horse into the distant eastern sky.

"Sing it again," Sarah said to him.

Hoggen was startled and turned around.

"Please, it sounds so sweet. Sing it again," she said.

"It is sweet and sad. Shall I sing it more sad or more sweet?"

"Sing it just the way you did," she said.

And then he sang it slowly, but in a loud voice.

> "It was in Donagal most green,
> her beauty was foreseen,
> Born so fair she was,
> But a promise she did make,
> To return, yes she must,
> Then left before our time.
> Well, it broke my heart, to see her go,
> Yes, it broke my heart
> Knowing she won't be mine.
> I see the billow white sails, now far away,
> No longer shall I see her face,
> But once I held this angel close.
> Then watched her fly away."

When he finished singing, Sarah's eyes were a bit teary.

"Mama Reena told me that there was a poster for you. Why didn't you say something?"

"Why? Because I can't tell you what I really feel. Now all I know is that I can't stay."

"But, where will you go?" she said, "How will you make it?"

"I . . . I don't know," Hoggen stumbled. "I'm a cursed man and I should leave before you get cursed because of me." Sarah grabbed him and hugged him tightly. They stood there unmoving for a long while like two statues embracing.

Then Sarah righted herself and took a deep breath and said, "I'll make you some food to take. Take the saddle and ride that Ghost of yours west out of here, you hear me?"

"I'm not going west," Hoggen said, "and I'm not taking the Ghost."

At that he jumped down and swung the gate to the corral open.

"What are you doing?" Sarah in alarm.

"I'm setting free what should be free." And at that, Hoggen shouted at his Ghost mare.

"Go on now, get. Be gone, ya. Fly." And he slapped her haunch and the Ghost jumped high on her two hind legs and shot out of the corral.

"But Hoggen, your horse is . . ."

"She was never mine. I'm doing this 'cause she saved Samuel."

Little clips of dust from her pounding hooves were the last they could see of the Ghost.

"I would be happy to take some food. I'm going to walk down to the river and head back down to New Orleans, but before I go, there is one thing you should know," and he grabbed her by the shoulders and brought her close to him, "I love ya. And your family. And I'll never forget ya."

Sarah looked at the red-faced man, and without saying a word, held him again in her arms, rocking slowly together in the morning sun, she said, "I know. I know," to the Irishman.

Later that morning, Samuel was up and about and watched in silence as Hoggen cleaned his sword, the Claidhim. When Hoggen saw him, he started in mock battle, stabbing, slicing and jumping back and forward.

Then matter-of-factly Samuel said, "Mister Hoggen, Mama said you're goin'."

Hoggen turned and smiled at the little boy.

"Aye, I'm going. It's time for me to leave. You're the man of the house now, Samuel. Do your Mama and Grandma proud.

"Are you leavin' cause they after ya?" Samuel said.

"Aye, they're after me."

"You gonna stab 'um?"

Hoggen laughed. "Only if they try to stab me first. Now get back and get some of those ash cakes for me that your mother's makin'. I'm gonna bundle them up and head on out."

"Mister Hoggen?"

"Yes, Samuel?"

"I won't never see you again, will I?" and at that his chin started quivering and his lower lip began to stick upwards towards his nose.

"Probably not, lad, but you know, any time you think of me in here," he said as he pointed to the little boy's chest, "and up here," and he pointed to his head, "then I'll be with you. Now go, get me those ash cakes."

Samuel ran back to the house and Hoggen could feel his chest tighten with emotion but he held it in, so the little boy would be strong, too.

Chapter XLV

The Run of the River

Rene and Abraham were on the focsle forestall of the Morning Star. Abraham was looking out as the big wheel turned the green water of the Missouri River white with its churning, and slowly pushed him back up toward his home. He had been telling Rene about his adventures.

"You know," said Rene, "I do not know if you've got the worst luck or the best luck of any man I know. In fact, you may have both!"

"Why do you say that," Abraham asked laughing.

"Because you get in more trouble and get out of more trouble than any man I've seen, and believe me, mon ami, I have seen many a man."

"Do you think Doc was able to tell Sarah that I'm alive?" Abraham asked.

"I hope he did or she'll drop dead if she sees you walking up the road to home, not knowing. She'll think you're a ghost, eh!" Rene laughed when he said this.

"It will be so good to be home," Abraham sighed, "Very good."

"Things change over time," Rene said, "Nothing stays the same." Then, out of nowhere, Rene said, "Abraham, I'm leaving. I'm done with this country. I'm going further west."

"What?" Abraham said.

"I've been thinking about it for some time."

"But what about your trading?"

176

"There are newer, better places for folks to trade now than my old post. Also, this country has become filled with people who want control. Want to control everything a man does. They want their own way of things that I do not agree with. I can't stay. New laws binding you into all kinds of anguish that pulls the life out of you. When I came here, the beaver ran heavy, we traded, and though many different peoples walked the land, we still found ways to live in peace. Now the beaver are gone, sidewalks of wood are built and now we've become 'civilized' like in the cities, eh," Rene spit. "It is not for me. No. I'm going to Texas with Doc."

Abraham said, "I don't know what to say." Then he spoke low and in earnest, "Except you are the second best friend I've ever had. I will miss you."

Abraham reached his arm out and clasped the hand of the big Frenchman.

"And I you," Rene said, "but you know you are like Lazarus, eh, my friend! I believe that perhaps we'll meet again."

"Perhaps," nodded Abraham.

The two stayed and looked out at the wide river listening to the sound of the riverboat swishing its liquid beneath it. Men stay silent like that when a moment between them has passed. A moment that will be savored in years to come, for men don't often speak what they feel, but they feel it nonetheless.

Higher up the river, at Rene's trading post, ten men of dark serious thought had gotten off another riverboat and first among them was Thornton. His knee high English riding boots tromped up the small hill, and even from a distance, he could see his posters tacked up outside the bar. He felt so close to finding Hoggen, he could taste it in his saliva.

"Soon," he said silently to his dead son, "soon, my boy, we'll get him for you. Soon, my boy."

Chapter XLVI

The Gold Coin

Dicey Morgan had built a saloon right next to Rene's trading post. Many's a man passing through that would stop to quench his thirst and pick up supplies to head further west. Unhappily, the farmers and the slave owners that came through weren't of the drinking kind as much as Dicey liked. Not like the deer skinned hunters and wanderers from before.

Sitting there that day on a bar stool by himself was old Mumbles. He was planted at the place like a cabbage in your garden. It didn't take long for one of Thornton's men to talk up Mumbles and for him being easy to liquor, to blurt out all he knew of the Irishman and the Cooper family.

A skinny, hollow cheeked Irishman with a bird-beak nose from Thornton's gang named Peters came running up to Thornton.

"I found him. He'll tell us everything, including how to get to the farm where Hoggen's staying. Money greases every wheel, hey Mr. Thornton?"

"Yes, you're correct Peters," said Thornton as he paid the gold dollar into the outstretched hand. "Bring him to me."

"I will, sir," he said.

"I'm sure it's 'im. Tall. 'im spends 'is time with negro Coopers. North, cross the ferry and follow the creek. Yeah. Follow the creek."

"Buy whiskey for this man. Thank you for your trouble, sir." And he threw another gold piece at Peters. Then he shouted to his men, "To the ferry, quick! I want to be across before the afternoon sun begins to set."

Doc saw the men and after they headed to the ferry, he said to Mumbles, "Who are they, Mumbles?"

"Them's the men lookin' for Hoggen. But didn't tell 'um nuthin'."

"No, by the smell of ya," Doc said as he smelled the whiskey on Mumbles, "Hoggen's closer to death than ever." Then Doc turned his back and went back to the trading post.

Down river, Abraham was a day away. He kept hoping that Doc had broken the news to Sarah and he kept going over in his mind what he'd say to her when he saw her.

"I wonder how big Samuel and Willy have gotten?" he said to Rene.

"Taller than you can imagine."

And he wondered who this Hoggen was that Rene had told him about. He hoped Sarah was okay, but he couldn't get over the fact that she of all people would have a white man living on the farm helping her out.

"I know she must have changed being a widow, and all." He said it like you do when you want the answer to be 'no'.

"Loss of your man and hard times will do many things to change you," Rene said, "But I know that I have never seen a woman love a man like she loves you. She has such passion, she could be French." And at that, both men laughed.

With every turn of the paddle wheel, Abraham felt more excited. "Home soon," he said, "I'll be home soon."

Up river, the ferryman's sons didn't like taking so many horses across and the Englishman was bossy, too.

"I don't like him much," Jeremy said to his brother, "Don't like what he's doing neither."

"Ain't our business what he's doing, Jacob, you just do as I tell you since Daddy's gone to help out that Cooper fella."

"But that's what I mean. Daddy helping the Cooper and now you lettin' these English cross, when you know what they're after."

"It's not our place, and we got monies to earn. They'd cross further north anyway if we didn't let 'em. We just saves them a few days."

"They just like the paddy-rollers," Jacob said, "I don't like them neither."

"You don't like nobody got business to do 'cause you so lazy."

"Am not!"

"Are too!"

The two boys continued their bickering when, as the sun was gleaming across the Missouri, Sweeney decided that this was the time to talk to Thornton.

"Mr. Thornton," Sweeney said, "If there's a chance, I'd like to talk to Hoggen before we have to use any . . ."

"What? Any guns?" Thornton said. "He'll come or die as far as I care," Thornton spat. "Listen, Sweeney, you don't dictate terms to me. I dictate terms to you."

"Of course, Mr. Thornton," Sweeney said nicely, "but you know, we still haven't got a warrant yet because we haven't found him and you just wouldn't want to have any complications, sir, would you?"

"Yes, Sweeney, yes. I see your point. Maybe I'll give you a chance to bring him to his senses. No reason to, ah, complicate things. Just the same, if he don't come, we'll be getting him anyway."

"Of course, sir, of course."

At that, Sweeney went back to the end of the ferry and watched as the two brothers steered her across the currents. Sweeney was a man of two goals. No one but he knew, until now, the secret that he hoped that somehow, when the time would come, he could keep Thornton from outright killing Hoggen. He knew that he would be the only one who could save Hoggen, and mostly, that he'd be the only one to try.

Chapter XLVII

Hoggen's Run

The pink skies of dawn painted the sky, the ground and the Cooper house in a faint grey/red hue and Hoggen stood and watched the dawn from the corral fence where he sat that morning.

"I should have left yesterday," he said out loud when Sarah came out to get some water.

"I'm glad you stayed. They boys need to see you. Samuel especially wants to say good-bye."

"I need to be off and catch the ferry."

When he had packed his sack and had wrapped his Claidhim, he gave Mama Reena a hug. Then he picked up little Willy and said his good-byes. Then he turned and looked at Sarah.

"I'll never forget . . . You saved my . . ."

"Hush, now," she said and put her finger on his two lips. "You get on and don't get caught. We'll be alright," she said.

"Will you be?"

"We'll be alright," she said with her voice cracking. "It's my farm, my land and you helped keep it that way. Now . . . it's time to get. Please take Judy."

"I can't take her, you need her here. I'll be fine, I promise."

Samuel came running up in his bare feet and his shirt flapping out of his pants.

"Hoggen! Let me walk you some, please?"

So the little boy and Hoggen walked past the farm and down into the ravine and Hoggen turned to him and said, "Samuel, it's time for you to go back now. Go on, boy. Let me give you a hug." And he squeezed little Samuel and Samuel handed him a little parchment.

"It's for you. It's my first letter. I can write a little now and I, I wanted to give it to you."

"I'll read it every night," Hoggen said. "Keep it up, lad, and teach Willy, too. You're the oldest and need to care for this family. You know enough now to get even better. Promise me."

"I will," said Samuel.

"Don't get killed, please," Samuel pleaded, "I loves you, Hoggen!"

"Aye, lad, and I you. Now go, our destiny parts us for now. Go! Now!"

And they touched hands and Samuel went running back, his bare feet slapping on the dry earth. Hoggen, alone again, turned, again leaving what he cared for most.

Hoggen could hear the buzzing of the insects as the sun began to heat the day up and figured he could spend the night in the open one more time before he got to the ferry to cross back to the trading post and catch anything heading south back to New Orleans.

Sarah was in the field when little Samuel came running up to her and jumped in her arms.

"Mama, everybody I love leaves. Why do they always leaves."

"Shush, now," she said, "everybody has to go sometime, now boy. But you always got family and you always got me."

And he heaved his sobbing little shoulders into her big arms.

"Now quiet down, I got work to do now."

"Samuel ran back to the house, blowing his nose on his long sleeves and Sarah fightin' back tears herself.

"Why does this happen, Lord," she said, "Why?"

Later that day, one of the hired Seminole trackers galloped his painted pony to the ridge that saw at it's opposite end the little farm. The men in Thornton's group galloped swiftly and Sarah, with a hoe in her hand, was startled when the horses galloped full speed up to the opening of their small front yard.

"My good afternoon to you, ma'am," said Thornton. "I'm looking for a man named Hoggen. Is he here?"

Sarah looked up but didn't blink.

"Who's looking for him?" she said.

"I am the father of a man, no, a boy, he killed. And he's wanted by the authorities. And there's a bounty out for him. A thousand dollars. It could be yours if you help."

"I don't take bounties and I'm not sure I know who you're talking about. What's this man look like."

"He's thin and tall. Has high cheeks, handsome, they say, in a boyish way, and talks with an accent. Some say he's been spending time here with you."

Sarah could see that two of the men were unholstering their pistols.

"How much you say is the bounty?"

"A thousand dollars."

"Mama Reena," Sarah said, "Man here want Mister Hoggen. Come on out, now, and bring your long rifle! Samuel, Samuel! Come here right now, boy, bring me some nails and that hammer."

Soon little Samuel came out with the nails and the hammer, but he looked confused. Sarah strode over to the barn and started nailing the door shut.

"Hoggen! Don't you say a word, now, you stay right in there!"

"He's in there, boys!" and suddenly their guns came out.

"You hold on, Mister! Mama Reena, are you there?"

"I'm right here, honey, and I got the long rifle pointed right there."

From the porch, Sarah could see Mama Reena holding up her rifle pointing, and except for the scary situation that it really was, Sarah would have laughed out loud, seeing her blind mama-in-law with a rifle pointing out to nowhere.

"Now you mind me," Sarah said. "I wants a thousand dollars, but even I know you gotta have some kinda piece of paper or something to take a man. Where's the sheriff? You go gets the sheriff and you can have this man. Hoggen, now don't you move, you stay right there!" Sarah shouted into the empty barn.

Peterson spat tobacco from his horse and drawled, "How do we know he's even in there? Maybe we'll just take him without a warrant."

At that, Mama Reena cocked her rifle, "We'll be burying you here," she said. "Now you get whatever my daughter says you gotta get."

"And the thousand dollars," Sarah said, "I want that thousand dollars."

"You'll get your money, Mrs. Cooper, if that's your name. Greene, these documents, take them back across and get a warrant from the sheriff in Booneville, now that we know he's here. Sweeney, now is your chance to go talk to him."

Two of the men galloped off with the papers and at that point, Sweeney walked up to the barn.

"I think I need to speak to him alone," he said to Sarah.

"He may not want to talk to you," Sarah said.

"He will, I promise. Hoggen!" Sweeney said, "tell this woman to come on and let you out. I swear, man, I think I can save ya. There's two witnesses that will testify for ya to say that it was just a fight and an accident. Come on out, now will ya? Come on out."

"You don't have to say nuthin' to him," Sarah said to the door, "Not a thing! You can stay there all day and not say a word if you don't want to, Mr. Hoggen." At that, little Samuel's eyebrows were raised and he cocked his head kinda funny when he heard all this commotion.

"Mama Reena," he whispered in her ear, "what's Mama doing? Mister Hoggen ain't in there."

"Be quiet, boy," Reena said to Samuel, "This is an old runaway slave trick. We just trying to make 'um think it so maybe Hoggen get further down the road. Worked real well on them southern paddy rollers."

"Oh," said Samuel.

Sweeney was getting agitated. "Hoggen!" he said, "for God's sake, man, speak to me. Speak to me!"

"He's not in there," Peterson said.

"You!" he pointed to the Seminole, "ride around to the back of that barn. See if you see tracks."

And at that, the Indian galloped his horse around back.

"Ma'am," said Sweeney, "if you're pullin' a trick here, that Mister Thornton's a mighty mean man to cross."

Thornton's patience finally thinned when he didn't hear Sweeney speaking to Hoggen inside.

"Open that barn now!" he said. "And you," he said as he pointed at Reena, "put that rifle down!" and two guns were pointed in her direction.

They pulled the nails out of the barn door and went through

186

the barn, and Thornton was fit to be tied.

"You liar! You . . ." and he raised his fist, but Sweeney stopped him.

"This isn't your place!"

"But we've spent hours!"

"I know, sir, but . . ." and then the Seminole came galloping back.

"Foot tracks, I found them, heading south."

Thornton's rage boiled over him and he pointed a finger at Sarah, "We're not done with this yet," he said to Sarah.

At that, Thornton and the eight remaining men galloped off.

As they galloped off, Sarah said, "Mama Reena, give me my rifle back and everyone get back in the house."

Sarah went and got extra cartridges just in case they came back. She knew that the worst was yet to come.

Chapter XLVIII

The Running of the Prey

Hoggen was breathing hard. Quick, shallow breaths as he swung his arms through the reeds along the creek. As he thrashed and crashed through cottontails, he zig-zagged and ducked and moved for cover as quickly as he could. He did so instinctively as an animal would who was being chased. He didn't know if at any moment he might be spotted by Thornton's men. Hoggen ran south. That's where he had to go. Not north or west, with no horse and no lead time, Hoggen had to take the river south and hope to get "lost" along the way.

As if his mind wasn't racing enough about where he had to go and where to hide, his thoughts kept returning to Sarah and the boys. For so long he had no one and nothing to hold onto. Now he did, but instead he had to let go again.

"Jesus, what a curse," he fumed out loud to himself. "First to run from me own land for killing another, then be saved by this woman, to love her and then have to run again." Suddenly he stopped talking out loud in fear that somebody might hear him.

Along the south side of the creek, Hoggen saw a sharp sided ravine. There was just a trickle of water running up it's middle, but looking back on the muddy tracks he was leaving, Hoggen decided to try and throw off anyone who'd follow him. First he walked along the creek and then doubled back in the middle of the water and when he reached the ravine, he carefully walked up the narrow fork, treading lightly so as to not show where he went.

He had hoped that his hunters, if they came, would see his footprints and keep following them down to the river and not realize he had doubled back.

As Hoggen walked up the gravel in the middle of the creek, the narrow ravine began to open up. "Must be spring fed," he thought as there had been no rain and yet the water kept trickling. There were wildflowers growing in the sides of the west bank. The flowers were a beautiful purple, lavender and yellow and they seemed a perfect picture. So different than the red and brown of the hills. The air smelled musty like water mixed with mud and then baked in the sun. It was as if all of his senses had been opened up by the fear running though his veins. All the time he had been with Sarah, he had never seen this place before. Now, it appeared as if he was entering a garden of some kind. A place that had been hidden from view before; a safe place, before the bad came.

He traveled about three quarters of a mile up this creek, and then it turned quickly. Climbing further up the creek, it turned into a pasture-like area that he thought must be under water during winter. But this time of year it still had green wild grass over two feet high. Surrounding the pasture, the cliffs rose steeply up 50 to 100 feet. Then to the west were little breaks where Hoggen thought the creek must continue. Butterflies were everywhere, flapping lazily and then landing on the wild flowers. Hoggen, tired and exhausted, decided to lay down in the grass.

In the wheat scent of the wild grass, his burning eyes slowly closed and soon he was dreaming of race horses and black mares on the coast of Ireland. His ship left and he said good-bye to his mother. There was the Ghost, galloping faster than anything he'd ever seen. Faster than Thornton. Faster than death. Her great strides outrunning them all and upon her, Hoggen rode. Free and tall, unbowed by the rich who hated the poor Irish. Faster than anything before. He and the Ghost racing through fields and everywhere were those he loved, clapping their hands in victory as he rode by them cheering him on to his freedom with the Ghost.

Hoggen did not know how long he had been asleep, but there is moment when a man is sleeping, that his dream seems so real, that it wakes him up, and in this case, Hoggen's dream woke him up. There standing directly above him was the snorting exhaling breath of the Ghost looking down at him as he slept in the pasture. He jumped up, startled, and she reared back.

"Whoa!" he said to her, "what in heaven's name are you doing here?" She shook her mane and pranced with her hoof in recognition and he patted her gently on the nose.

"Aye, perhaps you've come to save me," he said. "Yes, that's it. You'll let me ride you one more time." He continued to stroke her and talk to her, and as he did, her ears perked and her tail swished the flies and twitched, but he could tell she was relaxed. "How in God's name did you ever find me?"

Hoggen had no way to hold her, no way to ride her, except maybe to tie his red shirt around her. He looked at his shirt, took it off, and ripped it in two, and trying as best as he could to make some kind of bridle. She jumped when he put it around her neck, but then calmed again.

"Come, now, I don't want to have to break ya again. Be kind to me, sister, I swear I'll let ya go again if you get me out of this mess." Then she pranced and snorted some more, but she kept looking, looking over to the break in the pasture that Hoggen thought was a continuation of the creek. She was looking for

something, he thought to himself. Aye, but what she was looking for? Whatever it was, it hadn't come yet, and Hoggen hoped
perhaps that before it did, she'd see her way to helping him and
take him to his freedom. Suddenly, he jumped upon her back
and she took off like a bullet as they rode as one, to freedom,
Hoggen thought, "Please, my girl, to freedom."

Chapter XLIX

Almost Home

braham's mouth was watering so much that he spit off the side of the riverboat as it approached the landing. The familiar site of the trading post on the hill brought back memories of the first time he had laid eyes on the little buildings on the hill. But now new buildings had sprung up and Rene's Post looked old and shabby next to the new white washed ones. Even though the smoke from the boat's stacks blew south and east, Abraham was looking north and west as if he could see his farm, miles away. Rene stepped up and put his hand on Abraham's shoulder.

"You are lost in your thoughts again, Abraham."

"I'm just wondering. Wondering if even my Sarah will remember me like she used to," said Abraham.

"It is good for a man to be insecure in his love. We French never take love for granted. Love is a flower. You must protect her."

"If she thought I've been dead for so long, you just never know. Tell me," Abraham asked Rene in a hushed tone. "This Irishman, does he live on the farm with . . ."

Rene nodded in understanding, "In the barn. He sleeps in the barn. And he teaches your boy, Samuel, to read. And a horse-man, he is. Doc says he has the horse's spirit."

"Well, from what you've told me, it seems like he's got something if he a caught that thieving mare."

"Aye, and fast she is," said Rene, "fast as the wind."

Rene pulled out a bottle of whiskey. "Tonight we drink to your return, tomorrow we ride."

And at that, Abraham took a gulp of whiskey and choking on it a bit, laughed as Rene told him a story about how Doc once trapped a beaver and let it go in the trading post, then stood by while all the women in the place went crazy trying to shoo it out the door. The story distracted Abraham from his thoughts about his woman and how she might act when he came home.

When Rene was done with his story, he took another swig and said, "By the way, my friend, that is quite a handsome shirt. It looks Cherokee."

Abraham touched the red shirt with his hand, brushing it down the length of his arm.

"It is. It was given to me by Florence Comes-With-A-Feather, who I told you saved me."

As the night wore on and Abraham drank the whiskey, he told Rene of his last night with her, not knowing why, but needing to tell somebody.

"You can't feel bad about that," Rene told him. "She's a woman, you are a man. There's no shame in it if it's true between you and her. Here my friend. I drink to Comes-With-A-Feather who saved my friend from the river, then loved him, and clothed him and fed him too, so that he could come back to his family."

Abraham took the bottle in his hand and said, "To Florence Comes-With-A-Feather who saved my life and loved me."

At that, the Frenchman stood up and sang out loud, "Plaisir d'amour ne dure qu'un moment chagrin d'amour dure toute la vie."

Doc approached Rene's cabin and yelled at them, "Stop that ravel. You're waking up the dead spirits with that noise and scaring the fish from the river!"

Rene started giggling drunkenly as he greeted Doc, who had come back from a visit to his medicine field.

"By the way, Rene, what does that song mean that you been singing?"

Rene sighed, "It says the pleasure of love lasts only a moment. Grief of love lost lasts a lifetime. Eh, the French, we know love, do we not!"

At that, Rene fell back into a deep slumber. So, too, did Doc and Abraham.

The chill air of the morning slapped Abraham awake as the first bit of light came into the cabin.

"Up, up, Rene! We gotta go!" Finally, he thought to himself, finally he would be home if he could get the big snoring Frenchman on the floor next to him to help saddle the horses to ride. He could be there later that day if he could just get the big bear to roll up and move along.

It was Doc who finally poured water on the Frenchman to get him moving.

"Doc, how come you never told Sarah about me? I thought that you would! Abraham said.

"And tell her what? Tell her that you were charged with killing a man and they would kill you too. Then she'd of found that you'd died twice. It was better for her to think you dead, than to have hopes that you were alive and then to find that the whites would kill ya again."

"You a wise man, Doc," Abraham said, "but I hope she don't die of fright when she sees me."

"She's a strong woman. She's done a lot, seen a lot since you've been gone," Doc said, "You'll see." And at that, they went to saddle up horses for Abraham's ride home. On the way, Doc told Rene about Thornton's visit to the saloon.

Chapter L

In Sarah's Arms

Sarah woke up early, just as the new dawn was touching the rolling hills to the east. Two of Thornton's men were still camped out just outside of the farm, watching for Hoggen, so Sarah picked up her rifle and brought it with her. As she walked outside with a bucket to get some water, she looked around at her home, the farm that she had built and the fact that she felt so alone yet again.

"I sure hope Hoggen got to the river," she thought as she walked over to the creek to get some water. She wasn't going to cry about him, even though she wanted to. She vowed she'd never cry again after Abraham died, not for a man. But still, she felt an emptiness. She already missed the way his funny voice would almost sing words out, especially when he was teaching Samuel how to read. But it was more than that. She still had to figure out some way to get these men off her land, whether Hoggen was gone or not.

In the October afternoon, the sun was hot and she was sweatin', pushing the plow with old Judy takin' her paces in her usual way. Judy weren't much of a plow horse and was a better rider, but when Hoggen was around, she seemed to work harder.

The boys were helping Reena in the cabin. She was boiling up berry preserves and always made sure the boys got plenty of finger licks.

Sarah was bent, trying to free up the plow, when a horsefly buzzed her in the ear, and she instinctively swatted at it, shaking her head and shooing it out loud, and as she did so, she turned her head to see three riders approaching from the east.

From his horse, Abraham could see Judy in the field, and a woman bent over. When he saw the figure turn, Abraham spurred the horse, and off he galloped, leaving Rene and Doc behind him. His heart was pounding and tears were running down his face and choked him such that he couldn't utter a word. Sarah reached for her rifle when she saw the horse and rider galloping toward her, and because the sun was behind her in the afternoon sky, she knew she could get a good shot at him if she had to.

When Thornton's men saw the horse galloping to the northeast of them, they got on their horses, too, thinking it might be Hoggen who they could intercept. They didn't know who Hoggen was and they couldn't see exactly who the rider was, but anyone galloping that fast, they figured, was in a hurry for some reason.

As Sarah raised her rifle and pointed in the direction of the galloping horse, she squeezed one eye shut and focused on the rider coming towards her. As he galloped closer and closer, she could see he was a dark man and as she squinted, she saw a familiar look about him, but couldn't figure out why this rider would be galloping so hard towards her. Then, to her disbelieving eye, she swore he looked like Abraham.

Abraham saw her raise the rifle and choking through his tears, was yelling her name, "Sarah! Sarah!" he was saying. He was yelling louder and louder still, but over the galloping horse and her being so far away, she couldn't hear him. He started waving his hat, and when he took it off, Sarah could see that it was . . .

"Oh, my God!" she said, "Oh, my God!" She dropped the rifle and started running towards him and when he got about 100 feet from her, she broke down herself and started sobbing, and fell to her knees and Abraham fell off his horse, trying to get off too fast, and rolled in the dirt and got up and ran towards her. And with she on her knees, there they came together, Sarah screaming, "Abraham! You raised from the dead, man, you raised from the dead!"

"My Sarah! Oh my woman, I'm back," he said, and they clung to each other.

Abraham, his shoulders hunched around his woman, whispered in her ear, "My Sarah, I'm back." And they rocked together, swaying to and fro like two river reeds blowing in the autumn Missouri wind.

Thornton's riders stopped when they saw it wasn't Hoggen, then Rene and Doc came, and at that, the men nodded and rode off. Even ol' Doc had to sniffle his nose at the sight of Sarah and Abraham bound together.

Chapter LI

The Boy Say No

"Well, now, there they were, back together again. Ol' Abraham, Sarah, the boys and Mama Reena. That's about it.

"I think I'm just too tired now to finish up. Y'all come back tomorrow now boy, and I'll tell ya the rest."

"No, Grandpa!" I said, "No, no, please! Tell me what happens to Hoggen and all the rest. That man Thornton, too!"

I stood there with my eyes glued directly on my Grandpa's face.

"Naw, boy, I think maybe it's time to . . ."

"No!" There was a great shout from the room and all the fella's in their sleeping beds. All the old soldiers were awake. Everyone of them sitting up in their beds, because they had been listening to the story this whole time.

Hank Newton, who was Grandpa's friend in the ward said, "Y'all can't keep us in suspense like this now Hoggen. You got to tell the story. The boys can't sleep anyway because you've been talking so long, so finish tellin' your story!"

"Yeah," said Chris Bannion, "I want to find out what happened to that Irishman, and if there be any justice, I hope he kills that Englishman!"

"Ah, now, fellas," said Grandpa, "Let's not get all politicized about my family story, huh?"

"Come on, tell it!" they all yelled, "We want to hear it. Tell us some more!"

At that, my Grandpa reached across to get his glass and handed to me.

"You fetch me some water over there, Willie, and I guess I'll um, hmmm now, a where was I now?"

"Where was ya?" said big Yule Baney. "Your momma and daddy was on their knees huggin and kissin' for finally being together! What's wrong with you, old man? You can't remember your own stories?"

And at that, my Grandpa laughed and chuckled. "Just wanted to know if y'all was paying attention, fellas. Well, here is where it got real interesting. Yes, sir, real interesting . . ."

My Grandpa took a big gulp of water, sighed, and started up again, and all the fellas in the ward leaned forward on their elbows . . .

Chapter LII

Lazarus

O h, there was laughter that night, and crying. Reena was praising the Lord Jesus and all the saints and she cooked up all of Abraham's favorite foods while Rene and Doc listened to Abraham tell his stories about the battle with the white man and the Cherokee and the trial and through all the talk Rene and Doc sat mute and watched the reunited family.

It wasn't until later in the evening when the boys were down and asleep that Sarah and Abraham walked a bit in the Autumn night air. With the night crickets chirping, and there being a silence between the two of them, Sarah finally brought it up.

"You know about the man, Hoggen?" Sarah asked matter-of-fact.

"I know what Rene told me," Abraham said, "that he was a good man, and helped save my boy, but that the law was after him for some kind of killin' he done."

"He's a good man," Sarah said as if in defense of him. "Just bad luck follows him like water running down a hill.

"Abraham, you dying and now coming back is like Lazarus being saved, and he being here and then being gone just when you come. It's spooky."

It was like a bolt of lightening that hit Abraham in the head.

"My, God!" Abraham said, "Scrimshaw and them bones!"

"What are you talking about?" Sarah said, "What about them bones, whose bones?"

"Scrimshaw saw it in the bones. He saw it before it happened, then told me it would happen, too."

"What did he say?" she asked quizzically, "What'd the bones say?"

"I didn't really believe it, but now," . . . and he shook his head in disbelief. "Scrimshaw said there'd be death and new life and I'd come back different. Look!" And as he said this Abraham touched the side of his jaw bone which was now forever changed by the rifle butt of that paddy-roller.

"And you thought I was dead, and then I came back! It wasn't until you said Lazarus that I remembered. I remembered what he said."

"What did he say?" Sarah said.

"He said there'd be death, new life and I'd come back different and there'd be a man who'd give me rebirth and die and I'd give him rebirth. It must be that Hoggen. He saved my boy and I've come back and now that man's out to kill him. The bones must be saying I gotta help him."

"No you're not. You ain't goin' no where!" Sarah said as she grabbed him by both arms. "I'm not losing you again, even if Hoggen is . . . ," and she stopped, but her eyes betrayed what she was really feeling. "Even if he is gone, you're staying here with me. You're never going away again." Sarah grabbed his red shirt that Florence had made for him and held him tight.

Abraham said no more. There'd been enough emotion and shock for one day. On the hill they could see the fire of the two Thornton men like coyotes waiting for a kill. But Abraham knew what he had to do when he remembered the bones. He needed Doc and Rene to go with him to help find Hoggen, and if they could, keep him away from that Englishman.

"That's got to be what the bones meant for me," he said. And tomorrow, he'd make sure.

Chapter LIII

The Wild Herd

Hoggen and the Ghost were heading through a small opening away from the meadow as he did not want to go back to the river. The ravine, serpent-like, wound its way into the high plateaus, but to his surprise, it eventually opened up. It was a "back door" out of the ravine and when it opened, it opened onto the broad rolling plain.

The Ghost's strides were long, graceful and effortless. Hoggen was focused so far straight ahead, that he didn't know that behind him the Ghost was being followed. In the distance, the Seminole scouts of Thornton's group were following and Thornton's men had already reached the small meadow where Hoggen had spent the night with the Ghost.

In the rolling high grass, a high point could give you vantage for miles, and it wasn't until he had reached the top that he turned back to see that behind him there were two groups, the two Seminole scouts and behind that, another group of riders. He kicked the Ghost in her hind quarters to get her going again, but she raced in a direction he didn't expect, not going west, but south again. She covered ground like a hawk sailing over the prairie on a hot wind. She spat the ground behind her in huge chunks. Eventually, Hoggen hoped that he would be able to lose Thornton and his men just with her speed alone.

Amazingly, when she got to the gully, Hoggen saw the wild herd. Her herd. The one she built horse by horse for her stallion.

Her stallion was snorting and nervously ran around her when she arrived, unsure of what it meant with the man animal on her back. But the Ghost made some gesture known only to their kind, and she raced again further along the ravine. Then Hoggen saw the wild horses following the Ghost, and the stallion pushing the stragglers to keep up.

Once again, they rose up onto the prairie, thundering hoofs, a sound that will send chills down your spine if you was up close. The horses threw up great clouds of dust in a big fan behind their kicking legs. Hoggen was at the front of a wild herd trying to lose his man pursuers on the open prairie.

Thornton was back only five miles or so, still spitting with anger and his frustration at not having picked up Hoggen sooner because the Seminole guides had not figured out that Hoggen had back-tracked on them.

"You'd think an Indian would know an easy trick like that," he said to Sweeney.

"It's no matter, you'll still have him by nightfall," Sweeney said.

Shouting back at him, Thornton said, "The gold will clink in your pockets just as well as any Judas."

Up ahead, the Ghost was taking her herd as she pleased, but Hoggen didn't know what to do except hold on. That he did, figuring that she knew the land better than he and hoping that somehow, she would hide herself and her herd.

Eventually, she came upon a series of box canyons and ravines, and without hesitation, she steered Hoggen and the herd down and through a maze like series of cuts caused by years of Missouri rain and wind. When finally they stopped, Hoggen got off the mare but stayed close to her as her stallion was aggressive toward him and seemed like he wanted to get Hoggen away from the Ghost.

The Seminoles were good trackers, and waited until Thornton's men came to meet them at the entrance to the box maze before working further.

There was a trickle of water coming from the place where the Ghost had brought the herd. Hoggen, like the other animals on the hot afternoon, drank the water and thanked the Lord for his having placed it where it was. He knew his only hope of escape was to ride the mare wherever she would take him.

Chapter LIV

Sarah's Ride

A braham was sleeping, breathing the deep breaths of a man in his own bed, but feeling his arms somehow constrained, was awakened with the feeling of his two little boy's heads snuggled under each arm. He smiled and held them both tight. Shaking himself awake, he stretched and got up. He could hear his mama outside.

"Mornin', mama, where's my Sarah? Is she out in the field, or . . ."

"Oh, no, child," Reena said, "She left in the night with Rene and Doc. She took her rifle."

"She what!" Abraham said.

"She went to help Hoggen," mama Reena said.

"Why would she do that?" Abraham said, "I told her that . . ."

Reena held out her arms to stop him.

"Look, here, this woman been doing on her own for two years now. That man's her friend, and this her land, too, and her farm and her children done it all. And she ain't relied on you once. As I much as I love you, boy, you got to realize that you not the only one that's changed. She's changed, too. This land's changed her. Now you better stay here and take care of these youngins until she gets back, as I know she will. I know that you know why she had to go. So now, come on back and I'll fix you up some cakes, son." At that, Reena put her arm around her son's waist, and Abraham, unbelieving of what was going on, just shook his head and hoped that his Sarah would be okay.

It didn't take long when the sun was higher in the morning sky for Doc to figure out where the horse tracks were going and who was there.

"We're a half a day behind them, at least," Doc said to Rene, "You sure you want to ride this hard and this fast with that old Judy?" Doc said to Sarah.

"She'll ride! She rides a lot better than she plows."

Sarah knew why she did what she did. She sure knew she wasn't going to have Abraham get caught up in another mess, and she didn't believe them fool bones of Scrimshaw anyway. When she awoke in the night and heard Thornton's men leave, she knew they must be closing in on Hoggen. But she couldn't let whatever was to happen to Hoggen happen to him unless she tried to help. It was her choice, but now it didn't seem so bold, it seemed the right thing to do. So she, Doc and Rene rode on.

Rene, riding beside Doc, finally asked him, "Doc, you sure got a funny look on your face. What is it you do not tell me?"

Doc looked up in the sky and said, "A raven is flying. They fly to where there will be death, for they live on that which dies, as we all do. There will be death today."

Chapter LV

Trapped by Judas

Michael Sweeney and Hoggen were two peas-in-a-pod according to Sweeney's mother. Boyhood friends who ended up both working for Thornton. But unlike the others, Sweeney was hoping to save his friend if he could. It was Sweeney who paid the Seminole to tell him first when he'd found Hoggen in the box ravine.

The high clouds in the early morning gave a blue-pink glow as the sun rose. Hoggen was huddled, freezing, against the ravine wall, not even a fire to warm him at night, but at least with the Claidhim he was able to dig a shallow pit to curl up in. Hoggen was even colder for having given up his shirt, and all he had was his coat to warm him.

From above the ravine, the Seminole and Sweeney walked up to the ledge, and looking down, saw close to 100 horses sleepily prancing around in the misty morning air. Sweeney could see Hoggen huddled up, but was a bit too far to call out his name, so he crept down as carefully as he could, so as to not startle the horses.

When he got down to the bottom, he called out, "Hoggen! It's me, Michael!"

Like a spring let go, Hoggen jumped straight up, his body rigid in fear.

"Who?" Hoggen said.

"Michael."

"Are you with them?" said Hoggen.

"I'm here to help. Trying to save your skin. Now come peaceful, Jack, please! They've got laws here in America. You're entitled to a trial," Michael pleaded.

"Do you think that madman Thornton would ever let me get out of here alive?" Hoggen said, "You're crazy! You're a Judas, Michael."

"They don't know you're here yet."

"Of course they do. You led them to me," said Hoggen.

"Come peaceful, man. I swear they won't kill ya," said Michael.

"How much is he payin' ya? He is payin' ya, isn't he?"

"Of course he's paying me. You think I wouldn't take an Englishman's money to get me here to help ya? Come on, man, if it wasn't me here, it would be somebody else and at least you know you can trust me. Come along."

Hoggen was trying to survey what he could do to escape if he had to. Sweeney didn't have his horse, but he still couldn't tell who else was with him.

"I'll tell you what, Michael," Hoggen said, "Get your horse and come ride with me and we'll leave the Englishman to rot out here looking for me. You and I can start a life here."

"It's no good that way man, you know. There's only two ways this can end, and I want it to end the right way."

Suddenly Hoggen changed the subject, "Do you remember us on the cliffs of Moher?"

"Yes, I do," said Michael.

"I see you still got that old silly sword, huh?" Sweeney said to Hoggen.

"We had fun back then, as little boys."

"Yes, Jack, but these are the now days, man. Give yourself

a chance to live free in this country. Come back for a trial."

"He'll never let me go," Hoggen said as he shook his head. "Never."

And at that, Hoggen took his sword and ran towards the black mare. The Seminole, seeing him go for his horse, picked up his rifle and took a shot, just as Hoggen was climbing on the Ghost. The shot startled the herd and they began to wildly run about. Sweeney, taking cover, had to hit the wall or be trampled. Hoggen was just able to get back on the Ghost before she took off too, all racing and running around. But the mare, taking charge quickly, had them running out of the ravine and out towards the open plain.

Spitting out dust, Sweeney cursed the Seminole, but behind the Seminole he could see that Thornton and his men were up on the top of the ravine as well.

"It's over unless I get to him," Sweeney said out loud.

Chapter LVI

Where the Raven Flies

Once Doc had seen the tracks of a wild herd mixed up with the tracks of shoed horses, he started singing some kind of a song in the Osage language that Rene had never heard. Instead of following the tracks, though, Doc headed south and west and told Rene that if they were going to help the Irishman, they would have to ride through the night. That they did. At dawn, they, too, saw the blue-pink of the cloudless sky as the sun rose in the east and they approached the box ravines.

Rene said to no one in particular, "Do you know in Quebec we say 'red sky at morning, sailor take warning, red sky at night, is sailor's delight.' Perhaps it will rain today."

Doc looked over and grunted. "We could use the water."

It was then that they heard a gun shot.

Sarah yelled, "They've got him!" and kicked her horse to ride faster.

At that, Doc and Rene spurred their horses and galloped in the direction of the gunshot. As they rode through the tall grasses, they finally came to a high point and there below, less than a half mile or so, they could see Thornton's men, all with their rifles out, on the edge of a ravine, but not yet shooting at anyone.

Then, on the south end, charging up hard and fast, a herd of wild horses, and among them, on a black mare, was a white man whose pale chest was outlined by an open black coat flying behind him like a cape. He was holding on with a red cloth bridle, charging out and away from Thornton's men.

Sarah took out her rifle and was headed directly towards the herd.

"Rene, Doc," she said, "I'll ride and at least give him the rifle and maybe you can hold off Thornton's men for awhile, and . . ."

"Stop," said Doc. "This is not why we're here."

"What?" said Sarah.

"This is not why we're here."

"I'm here to save Hoggen," she said, "if I can."

And at that, she and Judy started riding towards the wild herd. Rene rode in the same direction, but Doc stood there, and opening his arms to the sky, started singing again.

Thornton was barking orders to his men, "You, head this way to cut them off, now! You with the long rifle, head to the top and if you get a shot at him, take it!"

At that, Lynch rode off with the long rifle to see if he could get a shot.

Hoggen was holding on for dear life as the panicked herd was racing away. Just as he thought they were making some distance, the Seminole met the herd head on and started firing at them, which turned the herd back towards Thornton. The stallion was running blindly, but the Ghost seemed to know what was going on and tried to cut back in the direction towards Doc, between the Seminole and Thornton's men.

Michael Sweeney had finally climbed to the top of the ravine and had gotten on his horse and was headed toward Lynch. Hoggen could see someone riding towards him with a rifle.

It was Sarah, and he was yelling at her, "No! No! Go away! Sarah, please!"

But even now, he was happy to see her face once more. As he screamed "no", he could feel a burning sensation in his side. It was sharp and hot. Looking at his pale, white skin below, he saw blood was pouring out. Lynch's carbine hit him true, and instinctively he jerked back the horse and they circled back in a wide arc, then the herd slowed down.

Sarah kept riding and was only a hundred yards or so away, and she yelled to him, "Come get the rifle! Come get the rifle!"

"Ride away," he said, "Please, ride away!"

And there was another bullet that whizzed over his head and he waved to her and took out his sword. The Claidhim. Yes, now he recalled what the old tinker had said to him years before: "Hold onto this sword for the banshee's blest it long ago. He who holds it cannot be defeated."

Hoggen raised up the ancient thing. It had been down this road before, he thought. She'd been gripped by the old chiefs and seen many a man die. Today he'd go, but with honor. His eyes were thin slits as he and the black Ghost rode directly towards Thornton's group, all of whom had their rifles raised.

And as Sarah yelled, "No! No!" off he raced directly toward Thornton, with blood spewing down his leg. The Ghost, smelling blood, her nostrils flared, she grew more wild and crazy. The other horses were smelling blood too, and they swirled in a panic, and followed their mare directly towards Thornton's group.

Up on the hillside, Doc, like a statue, stood with his arms raised up. Rene rode up next to Sarah.

"Shoot them white men," she said, "Shoot, them, Rene, shoot them!"

"Sarah," he said, "It won't do no good."

They watched as a parade of bullets came out of the rifles of the men in Thornton's group. Some hit the wild horses and some hit Hoggen. When the horses went down, the ones behind them panicked even more. Suddenly, there was a giant circle, and there amongst them, was Hoggen holding onto the horse by his one hand with the sword up high, and Thornton yelling loudly.

"Shoot that bastard! Shoot him!"

When he saw the blood coming from the Hoggen's chest, he cackled out loud and laughed, "That's for you, my boy, that's for you!"

The Ghost came within about 50 feet of where Thornton's men were. Hoggen's barely conscious body was trapped on the horse by his arm, and she, blood streaming down her sides, suddenly reared, and hoofs up high, started pawing, and charged Thornton with Hoggen flopping to and fro. Yet still Hoggen held with a vice-like grip, the sword swung out toward Thornton.

Thornton's horse was panicked and started kicking wildly and bucking. The Ghost's herd, by this time, was running though them all, and it was a great big, dusty horrendous display of men and horses. The dust was swirling like a tornado. Men being bucked from their saddles, and Thornton, screaming like a madman in a whirlwind.

The herd started trampling Thornton's men as they tried to escape this fury. Lynch and Sweeney were slack-jawed just watching the whole thing. So, too, was Rene and Sarah. But not Doc, for he was still standing up on the hill with his eyes closed and his hands upwards, singing some kind of song.

As the Ghost was running back and forth among the wild panic driven herd, she smashed directly into Thornton's horse, which lost its footing along the ravine. Thornton and the horse tumbled wildly down the side. Finally, the stallion took charge and raced off with the Ghost following him, dragging Hoggen along her side until finally, his limp body fell to the ground. His sword, now free from his grip, lay on the ground next to him.

Sarah had her hands over her eyes because she couldn't bare to see no more, except that there was a pain in her stomach like she'd been kicked.

"Why did I come to see this," she said. "Why?"

Finally, the panic slowed and calmed. Rene and Sarah rode off after Hoggen's body, with Doc trailing behind. Over their heads, high above them, a raven circled slowly.

Sweeney and Lynch rode down to find what was left of Thornton and his men. At the bottom of a ravine, they could see a dead horse and beneath it, the outstretched limp hand of Thornton. Sweeney couldn't help but notice that over the ravine, another raven flew.

Chapter LVII

The Horse Spirit

Sarah was crying and yelling out to Rene as they rode back to see Doc, "I was never going to cry again for a man. I can't help it now. I can't . . ."

Rene yelled back, "It's the lucky man that dies beneath the tears of a woman, Sarah."

When they met Doc, he was no longer chanting.

Rene said, "Doc, what were you doing, singing that funny song?"

"I was asking the Great Spirit to let Hoggen return. Return to his horse spirit. That is why he died out here. To return to where he was supposed to be."

Sarah yelled, "Stop that! He was killed by an evil man who . . ."

Doc shook his head, "No. Not all we see is all there is. He was a man, yes, but his spirit was trapped in a man's world. It is good that he returns. Let us get his body."

Rene knew not to say anything to Doc. Too many times over the years he had seen how Doc's logic worked.

"Hoggen was connected to the horses, Sarah. You saw it, too. Perhaps this is where he was supposed to go," said Rene.

"I won't have it that way," Sarah said. "It's always man causing his own bad end, his own fate."

"Maybe," Rene said, "but you are a witness to something very peculiar. I for one don't doubt it."

Doc rode off to where Hoggen's body lay. Sarah came behind with Rene. The herd was now long gone, with just a dust trail on the horizon of where they were going. As the three rode closer to Hoggen's body, they could see the Ghost also galloping back. The mare stopped when she saw that they were with him, and then turned and headed back.

"That's the strangest thing I've ever seen," Rene said to Doc, "It's as if that horse and that man were . . ."

"They are the same. She bears a foal inside her now. Soon the wild ones will be gone in the great lands of the west, as it should be," said Doc. "That is why he came here. A balance restored, the ravens have gone." Sure enough, as Rene looked up and searched the skies, the two birds had disappeared.

When Sarah got off the horse, she held Hoggen and closed the coat around him and said, "You poor, suffering man. You just never could get away."

Sarah looked up at Doc and Rene with her jaw and eyes set as to what she was going to do. "I want to bury him on my farm. He deserves that."

So they brought Hoggen back Indian-style on Doc's horse, Hoggen stretched out on a blanket between two poles. They didn't even turn to look back at what was left of Thornton's men.

After a while, riding up to meet them came Michael Sweeney.

"Get away from here, mister!" Sarah said as she raised her rifle.

"Please, please, let me say this. He was my friend. I was trying to save him, too!"

"Well, look at your friend now," Sarah said with bitterness on her lips, "No one saved him. I'm taking his body back to my farm. Not you or those other maggots will touch him."

"Bury him well, and here, bury this with him, please."

At that, Sweeney handed the sword, Hoggen's Claidhim, to Sarah and he got off the horse and touched his friend's body, saying a prayer. Then he got up on his horse, nodded a farewell, and rode away.

Sarah, Doc and Rene brought Hoggen back to the farm. With Abraham attending, they buried Hoggen on a little rise overlooking the river. Samuel, reading from mama Reena's Bible that Hoggen had taught him from.

In his little voice the boy read, Luke, Chapter 6, "Do not condemn and you shall not be condemned. Forgive and you shall be forgiven. Give and it shall be given to you. For what you measure, it shall be measured to you."

Though the winter was cold, the family was together for the first time in many a year. All through the nights, the boys listened to Abraham tell the stories of his stay with the Cherokee and he played his fiddle every night for them. Now far from all their troubles, Abraham watched in wonder as Sarah grew larger with a child.

"Now, Willie, that child growing in Sarah was me. Yes, sir, I was born in July of the next year. And on my birthing day, my daddy took me up to the grave where Hoggen was buried and named me Hoggen. He etched my birth date on the back of this here fiddle, just like he did with my brothers. So, you see, boy, that's how I got to be here so many years ago," said my grandpa. "That's how you got here, too, through me and then your momma and daddy who was my own boy."

At that, my grandpa closed his eyes and exhaled a deep breath.

"Now Willie, you the youngest like I was, and so this here fiddle ain't mine no more, it's yours, and it's your duty to be the

217

keeper of the Cooper fiddle and the Cooper name, and the stories that I've told ya. Can you do that for me, boy?

That I did, by nodding my head, and my Grandpa was just about to put his arms around me when in walked big Lucille, the day watch nurse.

"What in the Lord's name is this boy doing in this room with y'all?" she said.

At that, the fellas all cackled and laughed.

"It was ol' Hoggen tellin' a story," they all yelled.

"Git him outta here! Now! Shoo!" She waved her big arms at me and I could see them flapping like rolls of jelly as she did.

And all the men were laughing out loud for it was daylight and they had been up all night listening to Hoggen's story.

"Now, just a minute, Miss Lucille, if you please. Let me finish with the boy."

Then my Grandpa grabbed me and with his long arms, he brought me close to him. In a low voice he said, "And now you know, boy, you a Cooper. An American Cooper. Be proud of it and take this here fiddle, like I told you."

He handed me the fiddle and bow and the silk sack it was in and I held it close to me. But being young, I was still perplexed. Especially by them bones of Scrimshaw and all they was supposed to have foretold. So I asked him, "But Grandpa, them bones was wrong, then, huh? Them that old Scrimshaw rolled. 'Cause Hoggen was killed. There weren't no rebirth."

"Boy," my Grandpa said and he looked me straight in the eyes as he said this, "It was me that was the rebirth. I was the child of Hoggen and my mama's love and it was Abraham, my daddy, that raised me, for he knew the bones was right, too. Raised me to be special 'cause what was told to him. Said I had to keep the story alive and honor him and the man whose name he gave me. That I tried to do, too. Yes, sir.

"Now, go on, skedaddle, and get your mama, brother and sister and be on your way."

At that, my Grandpa gave me a big old wet sloppy kiss on my face and I tucked his fiddle under my arm and I walked outside down the hallway with my feet slapping on the hard floor and put my cap on my nappy head, just as proud and puffed up as a little boy could be holding my family's fiddle. Me now, knowin' we Coopers was a right fine family of Americans and I was to tell them tales to my family and pass 'em on just as I heard 'em. My mama and brother and sister were all asleep in the waiting room chairs and I had to shake 'em awake. Mama couldn't believe I'd been up all night.

Then me, my mama and my brother and my sister walked out the front door of that soldier's home. When the doors opened to the sunny winter's morn, I could see it was the beginning of a new year for us Coopers.

The End

Epilogue

"**B**ut Grandpa! Isn't there more to the story?" said Julie.

"Why sure they is, but I've been talking a long time."

"No, tell us," said Odessa.

"Yeah," said little Henry who was only eight. "Tell us more!"

Suddenly, from the other room, came Mary.

"William C! Are you still telling them stories about the family? It's Christmas Eve, now. The turkey's about to be carved and we have no time for no more tall tales about your family!"

"Come on, now, Mary, it's true! There's the fiddle, children. Right up there on the mantle. I'll play it for you after dinner!"

"No, you won't, William. These children are going to bed to get ready for Christmas morning!" Mary said in a stern voice.

Just then, my son, Abraham's great, great grandson Samuel, walked through the living room from the kitchen of his home on the west side of Chicago.

"Daddy, I'm sure the children would love to hear more stories, but it's Christmas in 1999 and your stories are always so long, it may be 2000 before you finish! Let's have dinner now and you tell them more stories later."

But Julia, Odessa and little Henry wouldn't have it.

"Tell us more, Grandpa, tell us more!" they all shouted.

"Why sure, I will, but first, let's eat." And thereupon I grabbed my cane, and slowly stood up and went over to where dinner was set at our long table. The long table of the Cooper family celebrating Christmas. I touched my Grandpa's fiddle as I passed by it, bringing back all my memories of listening to him tell me about our family. So, here we are, celebrating eight days before the year 2000, the American Coopers, with me cackling on with them old stories to my grandchildren, just as I promised that I would, that night to my own Grandpa.

Timothy J. Halloran
© 2005
Fiddlin Publishing 2005
www.grandpasfiddle.com

Cover Art by Dennis Anthony Augustus Dito 1998